The Man Who Would Be Kling

NewCon Press Novellas

The Man Who Would Be Kling

Adam Roberts

NEWCON
PRESS

NewCon Press
England

First published in the UK by NewCon Press
41 Wheatsheaf Road, Alconbury Weston, Cambs, PE28 4LF
February 2019
NCP 178 (limited edition hardback)
NCP 179 (softback)

Cover art by Peter Hollinghurst
Cover layout by Ian Whates

Minor Editorial meddling by Ian Whates
Book layout by Storm Constantine

One

Officially I was running the Kabul station as a clearing house, its status somewhere between an official embassy and a tourist office. Of course there were hardly any tourists, and the reason that countries saw no point in maintaining an official embassy in that empty land was the same reason I was rarely troubled with actual embassy business. Mostly what I was doing was keeping my eyes and ears open, and reporting back. Digital reception up there was most unreliable, and although cars and planes worked some of the time it wasn't possible to predict when they might suddenly stop working, which made the short hop over the mountains to Peshawar a nerve-wracking business. Peshawar was where I filed most of my reports, because it was far enough away from the Zone to have reliable data storage, and reliable communications.

Not that I tended to have very much to say.

When international bigwigs came to visit they tended to arrive via state-of-the-art dirigible balloon, so as to be sure not to plummet from the sky if the electrics suddenly cut out. But nothing so fancy was laid on for me. I flew over the Kush in a small plane, jets shrieking like dental drills, gritting my teeth with my two or three fellow passengers (usually military), and then I flew back again. Since the old Bagram airport was too close to the fuzzy borderline, a new strip had been built to the south-east of the city.

There was lots of room. The population of Kabul rattled around a city much too large for it: a weird patchwork of houses whole and ruined, some sectors flattened by war going all the way back to the Soviet invasion that had never been rebuilt. The UN mission was a four storey house, narrow and dark, with dust in-between the floorboards.

The early morning, when it's warmer outside a house than in, I would sit on my first floor veranda and let the sun warm me lizardly, and drink fresh yellow tea and listen to the noises. People going to work, vegetable sellers' cries, the occasional car, the lines of pilgrims who came to pray (for the zone, against the zone, it hardly mattered). It's one of the few places on Earth where there are no drones in the sky, which makes a pleasant sort of change. The only aircraft visible are small as gnats, crawling through the very high sky. There's a debatable ceiling to the effect, and a thousand metres higher a secure ceiling, and higher than that the UN and other agencies fly planes; observation runs, mostly, although what they think they'll see by plane that they can't see by satellite I don't know. Occasionally these very high planes drop bombs. Again, God knows what they hope to achieve. Knocking on some kind of door.

The effect of the Afghanizone on electronic machines is not predictable. You'll hear people say that it makes simple machines complex and chaotic, and makes complex machines moronic, or kills them outright. But it's not as straight forward as that. There are few electronic items simpler than a spark plug, but driving a car into the zone won't make your car a supercomputer: nine times out of ten the vehicle will simply die on you. Or it might explode. *Something* weird happens, of course, but exactly what is precisely the issue. So a drone might blow-up in mid-air, or might drop to the ground and not explode at all. Planes tend to drop unsmart bombs, antique ordnance, but at the height at which they fly there's no way of guaranteeing these bombs will fall onto their proper targets. Whatever those targets are. In a Peshawar hotel bar, one time, a very drunken woman called Sonia Kiazi told me the high command did indeed have a strategy, and that strategy was to bomb any geometric structure that hadn't been there the last time they looked. I asked: 'but why?' She lifted her shoulders and opened her eyes very wide and grinned, and burbled 'who knows? But we can hardly do *nothing*, can we. Can't just sit by and do nothing.' 'Geometric, like, what – buildings? Tents?' I asked. 'Landscape,' she said, wagging her head. 'Not hangers and pentagon-structures. Mountains. Features of the—' and then she was sick into my lap. She was a beautiful woman, but it takes more erotic desire than I possess to persevere in the hoursthat follow washing vomit out of my clothes and helping a retching, swearing, staggering woman up to her hotel room. I didn't see her again.

Sometimes these bombs stray perilously close to Kabul. You can hear them coming, a flute-like whistling sound that sinks to a pleasant C#. The hillsides around the city, and occasionally its ruined western suburbs, sprout gigantic cauliflowers of dust, and the impact communicates itself most intimately through the ground to your very feet. The windows bow and bulge inwards. From time to time we are shelled from other directions, although this is a rare occurrence and the ordnance shot by cannon or dropped by mortar tends not to provide the biggest bangs.

There's always dust. Bombing stirs up more of it. War, in essence, is the business of taking coherent structures of stone and concrete and milling them to fine dust.

Most days, though, nothing at all happens. Snow on the Kush feeds many rivers, so the fields to the south and east are well watered, and farmers do well. Some grow hashish and gene-tweaked opiate plants. They can hardly compete with the big operation in south west China, though, so this is small scale. A certain amount of UN money moves about, but since the electrics here are so unreliable conventional banking can't be relied on. There has been talk of printing an old-style currency for the country, but this strikes me as unlikely ever to happen. Back to paper scrip? Really? In practice an even more ancient currency circulates: gold and silver coins, and there's an elaborate system of IOUs that sometimes get driven down to Pakistan to get cashed.

One time my bosses sent me down to Quetta to 'liaise' (the word they used) with a damn-fool project to tunnel *underneath* the zone, and so discover how deep into the Earth it goes. I was to favour them with the benefit of my expertise, which amounted to pretty much gaping like a goldfish and looking startled, but who was I to argue? They'd tried it once at Ghazni, but the thing about the Afghanizone is that it pulses, sends out odd little tendrils of effect – impossible to predict when or where, and equally impossible to predict what *effect* the tendrils will have. An Iranian mining corporation, backed with big money from China and the US, had put a vast tunnelling machine into the earth west of the zone, and then the zone had borked it – so now howevermany billions of dollars of kit was stuck there forever. The new plan was to put in place a great many small-format diggers in positions all along the southern border. It was equally expensive and almost equally pointless, but that wasn't my call.

Anyhow, pursuant to this liaison they put me on a train from Peshawar running south of Afghanistan all the way to Quetta, and the joy of it was that, since I was on the southern flanks of the mountains, my Kindle worked. So I was able to read. And read I did.

There were half a dozen people in my compartment, and most were absorbed in the view through the wide windows. It was a pretty cool vista: light of impressive clarity and massiveness illuminating the southern flanks of the Hindu Kush. Nature imitating Rothko. Two passengers were having an excited conversation about the Rolling Stones playing Beijing, or at least the two of them left alive playing Beijing, heroically weathered as they were. 'The Eroding Stones', said one, and both laughed, though the other laughed more from politeness than hilarity. I tried to concentrate on my reading. But Chillingworth – I discovered her name later – slid into the seat next to mine. She was a tall, narrow-bodied woman with cheese-yellow hair, and prominent eyebrows the colour of purple grape.

'You're the Station Manager at Kabul,' she said.

'Can neither confirm nor,' I told her, without meeting her eyes.

Swipe left for a new page.

'I've a favour to ask you, friend,' she persisted. 'Concerning a man called Dallas.'

I looked at her then. The mountains rolling past behind her head, and the sunlight shaking off the snow at their peaks and parsing its magnificent glimmer everywhere. I looked back at my book without saying anything.

'I've been in your line of work, friend,' she said.

'My work doesn't run to *lines*,' I told her. 'Nothing linear about it, more is the pity.'

'I know whereof you speak. And Dallas is ex-army. Dallas is a he,' she added. 'Not the place.'

'Bully for him.' I wanted her to stop talking and to leave me alone.

Then she said, 'Darmok and Jalad at Tenagra,' and I realised I was going to have to help her.

'You been peeking at my reading matter?' I asked her, accusatory somewhat, but then I said, 'Shaka. When the walls fell.'

'Say rather, friend: Temba,' she told me, 'Temba. His arms wide. Say rather Mirab. His sails unfurled.'

I sighed. 'What do you want?'

'I want to talk a moment about my friend Dallas, and to situate him so as he might be *your* friend too. We're all part of the same Fandom, after all, and there might come a day when he might want a glass of Afghan tea and a half-hour chat on the terrace of your official residence, up in Kabul.'

'There's no need for the cloaky dagger,' I told her. 'It's a UN mandate. Your friend can simply apply to come.'

'He wants to go further than that. Upcountry.'

'Then he's bonkers.'

'Not illegal, though, I think? Such travel?'

'It's strongly discouraged. You want the lecture?'

'He's researched it pretty thoroughly. We have a plan.'

'You and he?'

'It's not certain whether I can accompany him. I'm hoping to. But if I can't make it then I'm hoping – look, look, I have no desire to *bug* you. I'll let you get back to your Diane Duane. It's only: well, if a heavily-built black man with a South London accent *knocks* on your door, you'll know who he is. Either way, your life will be long, you will prosper, and I *will* leave you in peace now.'

She moved to a different seat and I returned to my book. Just one more weirdo. There's no shortage of them. Then again, she was right about one thing: I had no grounds to look down upon Fandom. Fandom had been my tribe for many years. Lions and phasers and bears; oh my.

Anyhow, I went to my meeting in Quetta, and wasted my time, though not as comprehensively as they were wasting theirs. They listened politely to what I told them, which was a polysyllabic periphrasis of *don't bother*, and then evidently decided that I had been touched in the brain by some tendril or other of the Afghanizone, and ignored me.

I went back to my posting. Months passed, and I forgot all about my fellow in Fandom and her friend. She had said he would come calling.

He didn't show, though some others did. A high-profile Missouri webevangelist came to Kabul with the declared and crowdfunded mission (funded very generously indeed) to exorcise the whole of Afghanistan. It was the devil, this man said, the devil, running free because of mouse-lambs – I think it was – which improbable creatures had kept the blood of Christ out of the land. Hence the zone. This would come to all these benighted people, in time, he told me over coffee. The zone would; across Arabia and Malaysia and the wrong bits of Africa. It was the withdrawal of God's grace from the world, because of their heathen religion. This year, next year, the whole region would fall silent. He could stop it, though, with a properly performed exorcism. He was well-connected and I was advised to provide assistance, which I did. He blessed the whole land with holy water, and preached a lengthy sermon, and went away again.

Some military types visited. A new kind of drone – steam powered, it might have been, I don't know – was tested, and I assume it failed. They didn't tell me. Visitors were not common. Most of the months of the year, wherein no-one came to call, and the thermometer line twerked inch by inch up to the top of the glass, and my apartment was darkened to just above reading light, those summer months were a palpable oppression upon the spirit. The nights were very cold.

I got sick, and was feverish for a while; then I recovered. My cook, Ali, prepared delicious vegetable curries, and piles of fragrant rice steaming like dry-ice and hiding within its mound a great many almonds and raisins and nuggets of artificially grown protein. Then I would be lying awake in the small hours because the aircon refused to reboot after the last outsplurge of the Zone. Hot, hot. On the other hand, it never gets proper India-hot in Afghanistan, since there is too much cool air blowing off the Himalayas. Too much rain and too high a latitude. But in the summer it gets hot enough to wake in sweat, and lie there listening to the odd squawks and crunching sounds of midnight, softened by distance into melody, and to think: what's that? Is that – something? That is the dark half of the moon, and, as the advertisements say, 'it must be experienced to be believed.'

One Saturday night I was about to go to bed alone, if only I could summon the energy to haul myself out of the recliner on the veranda and up the narrow stairway to my room. The stars overhead were absolutely implacable in motionlessness, diamond pixels against the blackest shade of purple, and I watched them. From time to time one would slide slowly east to west – satscanning the area, I suppose. A door opened on the far side of the city and some strummy guitar music, probably live, spilled out, and then the door shut and the cicadas made the eardrums inside my ears shake and shudder.

I could have shrieked aloud.

Ali's shift was over, but he had not yet gone home. He coughed, in an embarrassed way. Someone to see me, he said. Sometwo, in fact.

I hauled myself up, and went inside; Ali lit a gaz-lamp to plump up the space with brightness, and the next thing two people stepped confidently into the little room. I recognised the woman Chillingworth, although she was dressed differently. The other I took to be Dallas. He was a foot taller than she, and dressed in an elaborate cosplay outfit. There was something wrong with his forehead.

They sat, at my invitation, and I poured some of the brandy I kept, since this was a UN property and not legally an Afghani house, and legally foreign territory, and so no insult was offered to the Prophet by the possession of such fluids, although we kept schtum about the existence of such a supply. I took a good look at the two of them.

'What we have to say, my friend,' Chillingworth announced, 'might well be of interest to you. For we two are going upcountry.'

'Both of you together? Insanity. You understand why that's insanity?'

'We have a plan,' grumbled Dallas, and leaned forward. He was wearing a blocky jacket, leather by the look of it, divided into panels. Over this he wore a sash that looked like two hundred rivets glues together, and there was a medallion round his neck a red enamel circle over which three curve-edged interlocking triangles were inlaid, a long vertical black knifeblade shape and two stubbier blades flowing down and away left and right. Naturally I recognised it. But the most impressive part of this outfit, coming clearer to me as he leaned into the light, was the forehead: two parallel lines of ridging marched like a topographic map of mountainous country up his high brow.

'It's no prosthesis,' Chillingworth told me, with satisfaction. 'Not a rubber forehead glued over his old forehead. My ears, neither.'

I looked again, and saw that her ears had been surgically altered to give them the shape of a poplar leaf.

'They put lines of a sort of biogel,' she explained, nodding at Dallas' head, 'which is a genetically engineered material grown from a sample of your own cartilage.'

'Hurt,' growled Dallas, sounding very unlike the culture to which he had decided he belonged, 'when they stuck the needle in, I can tell *you*.'

'It's his actual forehead,' Chillingworth clarified, 'is the point. It grows into a unique pattern based on your underlying bone structure and so on. It's real.'

'Real,' I said. I looked at them again. 'So are you a – couple?'

They looked at me then, and both of them had exactly the same expression. Though no words were spoken their faces communicated in unison two distinct syllables the first *puh-* and the second *lease*.

'Friends, then?'

'Fellow fans,' said Chillingworth, 'in the same fellowship as yourself.'

I took another slug of brandy. 'There's an official spiel,' I told them, 'but you know what? I'm going to spare you that. All I shall say is: don't go. People who go upcountry never come back, or more rarely they come back with severe mental impairments. If you go inland then you're on your own. We can't come in after you, no air ambulance can fly through to pick you up. All I shall say is: there are much more pleasant ways to kill yourself, if killing yourself is what you've decided upon. Your bones will bleach under the Afghan sun until somebody figures out how to turn the zone off, and who knows when that will be.'

'We won't die,' growled Dallas.

'Sure,' I said. 'I get it. Those others were weak and you're – I get it, I truly do – you're *strong*. But the zone doesn't care about that. Strength is irrelevant to it. Weakness likewise. Hope is irrelevant. Curiosity is irrelevant. There's *nothing* there. No man needs nothing. That's the point I'd like most to stress, actually: there's nothing to go questing after. There's no *there* to get to. No there, there.'

In a previous era there would have been government fences preventing entry to the zone, at least some of the way around it. But the political logic nowadays is permissive, and I'll tell you for-why: because it's cheaper. Fences are expensive, and so are guards, and so is incarceration and the issuing of passports and all that. Let adults do what they want. They want to walk to their death? Up to them.

'Friend,' said Chillingworth. 'We know what we're doing.'

'The others who have ventured into the Afghanizone,' said Dallas, in his low and rumbly voice, 'were human beings. What happened to them happened *because* they were human.'

'And you're not human beings,' I said. I meant it sarcastically, but somehow it came out as simple endorsement. Chillingworth smiled thinly, and nodded, and the whole shape of their crazy fantasy came clear to me in an instant.

There are various theories about the zone, as of course you

know; but three have the most purchase. The bald fact is that nobody *knows*, and it's proving very difficult to garner the kind of useful data that would diminish our ignorance. But of course people have theories. The leading theory, if I can put it that way, is that the zone is an artefact of war – some weapon that no government will officially confess to having developed, some unintended consequence of experimental battlefield tech, something along those lines. The most obvious consequence of the zone is that it interferes with electronics in unpredictable ways. It will mostly shut electronics down, but on occasion it will, shall we say, monkey around with electronic-based technology. The circuitry and programming of complex machines may still function, but in radically reworked or dumbed-down ways; simple circuits may suddenly acquire fractal complexity and come alive. It's deeply odd. Many experts think that all this is the consequence of some weapon designed to attack electrical operation. Then again, nobody is quite sure how it would work, this weapon. I once spent an afternoon in a Mumbai airport bar with a young military officer and she told me *her* theory. Since the zone is, empirically, operational (she said) then there must be something inside generating this effect. 'But one day,' she said, 'a high plane will drop a bomb and knock that whatever-it-is out, and then the zone will switch off and we'll get all that real estate back – not,' she added, lifting her wine glass 'that we're really missing anything by being deprived of it.'

'Cheers,' I said and clinked her glass.

Since human consciousness is, fundamentally, an electrical activity, entering the zone has unpredictable consequences on live test subjects. There are ethical problems in sending even volunteers in, even if you're only sending them a couple of hundred yards with a rope tied to their ankle, so they're easy to retrieve. The EU sent in some chimpanzees, apparently: simians who had been trained to use sign language. But they all died.

At any rate, that's the closest thing we have to an 'official' theory. A second theory is that the zone is something natural, some excrescence from the landscape, some hitherto unknown blip in the Earth's electromagnetic field, or something like that. The problem here is that, well, there's no precedence for it, no evidence for such a blip and no explanation as to how it could have come about. But there are perfectly reputable scientific conferences on the subject, trying to link the phenomenon to the Tunguska event or the periodic switches of north and south poles or whatever.

And then there's the third theory, which, evidently, was the one in which Chillingworth and Dallas had invested. Aliens. But 'aliens' is even more of a black box explanation than the Earth's mysterious electromagnetic whatnot or secret superweapon X to which no government will own up. And aliens, as explanation, attracts a certain kind of nutter.

'What we can offer you, my friend,' Chillingworth was saying, in what I now recognised as a voice aiming for a level rationality of tone, 'is knowledge. The most precious commodity of all.'

'If you come back,' I told her, 'then your main business will be figuring how much saliva to drool.'

'That might happen to humans, see,' said Dallas. 'But we ain't humans.'

'The way I figure it, the zone is an invitation,' Chillingworth said, beaming a smile that struck me as, frankly, lacking in logical dispassion. 'From *them*. The mistake we have made, hitherto, is in believing that human beings were the ones being invited in. But why would *they* need to create a special zone just to invite in human beings? Human beings are everywhere.'

'Ever'where,' agreed Dallas.

'Common as weeds. I think *they* are not interested in what we are. I think *they* are interested in what we can become. And what we can become is other than humans – more than mere humans.'

'No offence,' drawled Dallas, and grinned. He had had all his teeth replaced with sharp little sharktooth pegs. Must have cost a fortune.

'So you'll come back, with the key to the mystery of the zone,' I said, 'and in return you want, what? Bars of gold-plated latinum?'

Once again with the Dallas's rake's-teeth grin. 'One or two wouldn't go amiss.'

'Really we're offering you something *very* special,' Chillingworth said. 'First access to our knowledge. After you, and the UN, then we'll be V.I.P.s, globally speaking. We'll be the ambassadors for the next stage in human evolution! We'll bridge the earth to the stars! Queens. Queens and Kings, all of us!'

'*You* can talk to the powers that be,' Dallas urged. 'Arrange the, you know. The appropriate.'

'Maybe a private jet,' suggested Chillingworth. 'We'll probably need an apartment near the UN building. We'll need a publicity person, a handler for the press and such – because when we come back every media outlet in the world will want to talk to us. But *you* can say we went in under your aegis!' She brought a tablet out of her backpack.

'Risky,' I said, 'bringing one of those in here. We get small-scale interference from the zone all the time, and it fritzes equipment like that.'

'Oh, we're not taking this upcountry,' she replied, as if she hadn't heard me at all. 'We only need you to autosign.'

I glanced at the 'contract'. Was there any point in telling them that it had no legal standing whatsoever? I shrugged, signed. It included a clause on film rights, bless their hearts. I tried one last time to save their geeksome lives.

'Let's talk about this again over breakfast,' I said. 'Do you have somewhere to stay? We do have guest rooms here, if you're in need.'

'We wouldn't presume,' grumbled Dallas, his immensely

bushy eyebrows deepening their V.

'Thank you, friend,' Chillingworth assured me, earnestly, 'but we have rented a house on the Kuchi Murgha.'

'It means Chicken Street.'

'We have done,' growled Dallas, 'our research.'

His tone irked me. 'Make the most of it,' I told him, 'because once you go upcountry your brains will be turned into slushie, and all that research won't mean jack rabbit.'

'Good night, friend. Have a word with your superiors,' said Chillingworth, getting to her feet. 'They'll be excited. *We're* excited.' I was silently willing her not to say *make it so*, but she added: 'make it so!' and they clonked down the wooden stairs and passed out into the night.

The next morning I felt bad about being so dismissive of them, and worried that I hadn't done enough to try and persuade them out of their suicidal idiocy, so I put on my boots and went out into the cool morning. It didn't take me long to locate them. There are fewer shopkeepers on Chicken Street nowadays than there used to be, but visitors still do sometimes check out the lapis lazuli trinkets and authentic Afghani rugs. Two crazy Westerners, one *iswadda*, both in fancy dress, oh yes sahib, they hired a room over Sadar's shop I believe, thank you, no thank *you*, and I was knocking on the street-door and Chillingworth, still in cosplay, was leaning out of the streetside window and telling me to come right up. So I went right up, and made my peace with the two doomed souls.

Dallas' augmented forehead looked even more impressive by daylight: a huge Mars bar melted into the structure of his skull. Dust sifted down through the gaps in the ceiling-boards. Somebody upstairs was singing tunelessly in Farsi. Sunlight through the window tunnelled a shaft of beauty out of the impure air.

'Mr U.N.,' Chillingworth exclaimed, and showed me her right hand, on which she was counting 2 fingers + 2 fingers + 1 thumb. Which adds up to *oh for crying out loud.*

'I'm sorry if I was short with you last night,' I told them. 'You're still set upon going upcountry, then?'

Dallas showed me his full set of wide-spaced shark teeth. Chillingworth said, 'It would hardly be logical to back out now. We have bought two mules.'

'Well, I admire your courage, my friends,' I said.

'It does not require courage to buy mules,' Dallas growled. Then he made a series of noises like somebody choking on an unchewed segment of toblerone, which display of linguistic accomplishment made Chillingworth smile broadly. 'You are worried, Mr U.N. You should not be. *They* will recognise us for what we are. And *we* are no longer homo sapiens.'

'Funny things happen to animals upcountry,' I said, trying my best not to sound too offputtingly automatically negative with regard to their suicide mission. 'You've done your *research*, so I'm sure you've read about it. They go crazy, sometimes they die. Often,' I corrected myself, 'they die.'

'It is an interesting question,' Chillingworth agreed, putting all her left fingertips precisely against her right fingertips and circling her thumbs about one another. 'After all, electricity is part of the natural world. Insects, say, they have nervous systems, don't they? Are they all killed, or strangely complexified, by the Afghanizone? Does lighting never strike in this territory? According to the Rabbi of Jerusalem, electricity is a fire inside every single atom – does the landscape itself decompose and recompose according to its own logic in this place? No!'

'At any rate,' I said, rather regretting coming, and deciding it was time to leave them to their fate. They were adults, after all. 'I wish you luck.'

Before I could go, Dallas insisted on showing me the contents of his saddlebag. The most unmissable element was a two-yard-long piece of sharpened metal, shaped like an art nouveau reindeer antler, with two inset hand-holds upholstered with pads of leather, so that the thing could be grasped without slicing one's fingers off. He gave me a quick demonstration, swishing it alarmingly around the confined space. He assured me that *it* required no electricity to function.

'Bat lathe,' I said. 'Yes, he never did like guns, did he, old Batman.'

Dallas's epically crumpled and ridged brow crumpled a little further in puzzlement. 'No no,' he said, urgently. 'It's got nothing to do with *Batman.*'

'I know,' I said. 'I was joking.'

'You were,' he returned, in a dangerous voice, '*whatting?*'

Chillingworth put her hand on his arm. 'It's Okay, Dach'las. He is one of us.'

'Besides,' Dallas grumbled, fitting the blade back into its saddlebag. 'We *also* have guns.'

'Which,' Chillingworth hastily added, 'we earnestly hope we will not need. We are on a mission of diplomacy, to meet with the creators of the zone as equals, one to one.'

'And good luck with that,' I said, and left them.

I caught one last glimpse of them making their way up the Salang Road, the mountains before them, peaks dusted with a great many sieve-shakes of new snow, fine and tempting as sugar. The sky was that unearthly blue you don't see in any other portion of the globe, although presumably it's the same sky stretched over us all. Unclouded. Blue as your first-love's eyes. Blue as a primrose during a luminous dusk. Uncountable acres of pure blue over everything.

Two

I was on my way to the University, or more specifically to the UN communications hub – an eight-metre by eight-metre room staffed by one person on Mondays and Tuesdays – which was where I filed my preliminary reports, and logged all upcountry tourists. In my early days of the zone there were plenty of tourists in Kabul; or at least plenty of sightseers, scanning the distant mountains with all manner of sight-magnifying technology. You could sometimes see the corpses of people who had strayed into the zone, lost their minds and wandered around until thirst, or a fall, or a snake bite (or whatever) had killed them. You could make out the ruins of abandoned houses, some close enough to count as the suburbs of Kabul. It was very rare to see movement, although kites occasionally circled through the air, and once in a while a wild fox darted across scrubland, like a flame running down a fuse. But the flow of people diminished, since there was, really, nothing to see, and nothing to do. In the early days many foolhardy or tomhardy types ventured into the zone, and some died in full view of the people watching, and some made it to the mountains and died there. It didn't take long for the numbers of people ready to attempt so perilous a trip to fall away.

Still, I had my orders. Any people proposing to enter the

Zone were to be logged. I should restrain them only if they were patently sectionable, or a danger to others. But if they seemed rational enough then the UN operated a permissive policy. Sometimes folk came wearing home-made protective gear they were confident would shield them from the zone: white-haired absent-eyed men, mostly; men of the 'it's my own invention' type. Sometimes they relied on the power of Christ, or on special oils rubbed into their skin, or a map downloaded (they stressed) from other dimensions that promised routes of safe passage. In each case I tried, in a more or less desultory manner, to dissuade; and when I failed I reported them to the section chief, who logged them. Satellites observed their passage, I suppose; or high-flying spy-planes, and how far they got and in what manner they died was impartially noted down. It was data of a kind, though think about it for a moment and you'll see that it is all the same data.

This being neither a Monday nor a Tuesday the comm-hub was empty, so I phoned through the details myself. The hand-crank on the phone goes round-and-round, round-and-round, round-and-round, crank on the phone goes round-and-round, round-and-round, all day long, or so it seemed. Then: 'Hello?'

'Hello. I'm reporting two tourists entering the Afghanizone.'

Then: 'Wait it's buffering, what is this slow motion replay something, this is no use. Piece of crap machine. Wait till I get a pencil, or a pen. A pen or -cil. *There* we are. So?' Crackles and fizzing on the line made it quite hard to follow his words.

Names, identifying features, last seen location. I added, 'They're dressed as space aliens.'

'Anus did you say?'

'Aliens. One in grey, the other in a sort of black and gold number. They reckon that E.T. is behind the zone, you see, and that by becoming aliens themselves the zone will leave them be.'

There was a weird repeating clicky noise layered over the hissing and fizzing. It took me a moment to grasp what this new noise signified. It was the man at the other end of the line laughing. Cruel, really.

And that was that. I got on with my duties, and heard nothing more about Chillingworth and Dallas. About a month later I did my stint at the annual Zone conference, in Neuchatel, Switzerland. In the early years of the phenomenon this conference was a huge jamboree, with saturation media coverage and days and days of papers and press-conferences and scientists in low-ceilinged bars discussing the ramifications of this and the likely causes of that, strategies for containing it if containment proved needful (it didn't), strategies for eliminating the zone, if the state powers of the world decided such an approach was justifiable and achievable (it isn't). But year after year the conference met, and the amount of knowledge we accumulated about the zone, as a species, plateaued, and moreover plateaued at a very low level, and there was nothing more to say. By the time I was sent, covering for somebody more important than I who had better things to do with his or her time, it had shrunk to a two-day small scale going-through-the-motions exercise. There was nothing to say, and a few groups of bored people said it. At any rate, I was instructed by my bosses to attend this conference, and so I sat through four or five terribly dull presentations, and afterwards drank *kir* with an attractive EU official who casually dropped her marital status half an hour into our chat, leaving me to wonder if this was a come-on, or a back-off. 'You handled the two space alien folk, didn't you?' she said.

'I'm not sure *handled* is the mot juste.'

'Emoji, did you say?' The bar was playing 'Sympathy For The Devil' (the Motorhead version) and the conversational acoustics were not good.

'Mot,' I said, loudly, 'juste.' So much for impressing her with my *français*.

She said, 'I saw the surveillance footage from that case, you know?'

This was actually interesting. 'Oh yes?'

'Satellite footage. They got quite a way inland actually, further than almost anybody else – more than two, and nearly three kilometres.' Precise measurements of distance are not the idiom of the zone. 'Then they vanished.'

'Vanished?'

'Gone, like breath into the whatsit, wind is it? *Disparu.*'

'Does that often happen?'

'Oh,' she said stretching in her seat a feline way. 'It was just two dots really. But we traced them all the way into the zone. No, wait, that's not it. They were on horses, or something, so not dots. Rice grains, say, moving awful slow over the landscape. Then: gone.'

'Beamed up, perhaps,' I said. She assumed I was joking, and made thereby an ass of her and, I guess, of me too.

'It'll probably be that they fell into a hole. Rice grains isn't right; baked beans. Big enough to see some detail, but maybe our target slips into a hole in the ground, or gets dragged down into tall grass by a predator and eaten.'

'Not very likely, that, in the highlands of Kafiristan,' I noted.

'Or quicksand. A cave – there are a thousand reasons why they might just pop off the surveillance. Anyway, they vanished, and they haven't been spotted since. Dead I guess.'

The perky way she said this rubbed me up the wrong way. It's no laughing matter, really, death.

In the event, my new friend was playing the arm's-length tease game, and when I tried to insinuate myself closer she reminded me that she was married and kissed my cheek with a tragically serious expression on her face, and went off. So I went back to my hotel room alone to watch CNN. Poor old Chillingworth, I thought. I was less heartbroken by the fate of Dallas. He had struck me as something of a brute. Callous of me, I suppose. Conceivably racist too.

I had two weeks off, and went home. After that I was in

Tehran for a month, and I was not on the rota to go back up to Kabul for another half a year, except that the station officer got bitten by some insect that left them with a fever hot enough to cook crumpets on their naked skin, they said, and lesions on the brain (and early retirement), so they flew me back up to Peshawar, and I rode in a bus back to the old city. In one sense, better than flying over the mountains; in a series of other, boneshaking, sweating, headaching senses, rather worse.

Three

Returning to Kabul felt like a homecoming. First time it had ever felt like that, I have to say. At any rate, Alí was pleased to see me. He hadn't been sure when I was coming, and had no supplies for supper, but it didn't matter. I ate in one of the cafes on Chicken Street – Sharif's it was: I recommend it – and renewed my acquaintance with the proverbially hospitable Afghanis, or at least with that remnant of their people not diaspora-ed all across the world by the advent of the Zone. And the sky overhead slid the colour bar right-to-left on an epic scale from pale blue to straw yellow and tangerine and coughsweet red, and the sun went down in glory. Birds of prey circled in the dusky air, and bats grew bold enough to come out and to zip through the air like shuttles on an invisible loom. The scent of jasmine and frying wild-onions and diesel possessed the air.

I said goodnight to the people in Sharif's, and wandered without haste back towards the UN house. And there, on the road, was an old beggar, like a historical re-enactor from the nineteenth-century. He was wrapped about with a filthy cloak, much too big for him, and when he got up to follow me he moved his feet one over the other like a bear. He was bent into an r, his head practically sunk between his shoulders – this rag-wrapped, whining cripple who addressed me by name, crying that he had come back. 'Can you give me a drink?' he whimpered. 'Thirst is impairing my logic.' Croaky though it was, I realised that the voice was female.

It was only then that I realised Chillingworth had returned from the Zone

'Chillingworth!' I cried. 'Chillingworth, Chillingworth – you're alive.'

I helped her back to the UN house. She coughed the whole way, a scratchy strained sound like a fox-cub's bark. At One point she fell to the ground and I had to help her up.

Inside, I sat her at the table on the ground floor, since stairs seemed pretty strongly counter-indicated by her broken-down physical condition. She panted and gasped and struggled to get her breath back. I offered her the last of the brandy, but she mumbled something about how there was no alcohol on her home world and she wouldn't sink so low as to start drinking like a human. I opened a new bottle of water and she drank some of that, then she said, 'But I'm *half* human, of course I am. Why would I deny my heritage? Maybe I will have a snifter of that brown distillation, that alcohol liquid,' and she started coughing again, shaking dust out of the seams of her ragged cloak as she did so. Over and over the cough repeated, like a glitch in a recording. Finally she controlled it enough to take the glass of brandy in her right hand, and I saw that her fingers had been deformed, or twisted, or burned, or something. What?

'Chillingworth,' I said. 'Where's Dallas?'

And at this she looked at me with a weird intensity, and then she hoiked up a kind of kitbag onto the table, and it thudded onto the wood with an unpleasant solidity, as if it had a small bowling ball inside.

I did not want to look inside the bag.

'My God, woman,' I cried, practically shouting at her. 'You survived! You went into the Afghanizone and came out again, and you're – you're –'

'Changed,' she rasped. She put her head down on the table and slept, but for no more than a minute. I went through to the other room, and luckily the phone was working. So I called the medical centre and asked them to come to the U.N. house and attend an urgent case. *On our way,* they said. *There in a jiffy.* I went back through and watched her.

She woke with a start. 'I've never stopped to just *look* at clouds before,' she said. 'Or rainbows. You know, I can tell you exactly why one appears in the sky, but considering its beauty has always been out of the question.' Then she started coughing again, but in a new way, a shorter, more musical series of hiccoughy noises. It took me a moment to realise that she was weeping.

'Chillingworth,' I said. 'I'm going to get a doctor to look you over, alright? Why don't I help you upstairs and you have a lie-down, and in a bit we'll get a medic to look you over.'

'It is alien mariner and she stoppeth– do you *remember* me?'

'Of course I do!'

'Listen. Give me more brandy and listen.'

'That's the last of the brandy.'

'The doctor will have some, won't she? Doctors carry brandy don't they? For its medicinal – medicinal – purposes of – though my species does not consume synthenol. But this would be the real thing, wouldn't it? Where was I?'

'You're a bit scattered, mentally,' I told her. 'But you're the most compos mentis of anyone who has ever been inside the zone, and come out again. This is huge – this is really huge.'

'Listen,' she said. 'We rode our donkeys up past the old airport, ruins now of course, with the mountains on our left, and we kept going. Kept all the way along. Do you think it a coincidence that the zone drew its borders at the site of an old airport? It's about travel, isn't it. Going and coming, technologically augmented coming and going. Boldly going. We went. Dallas was all bravado, at first. Today was a good day to die, he told me. More than once. But it soon grew hot, and he was sweaty inside his cos-.' She made a kind of strangulated noise.

'Costume?'

'Uniform. But then we took the road up through the mountains, aiming to go up and over, and near the top it got horribly cold. We had winter coats and gloves and hats in our luggage, of course, and we put those on, but I got a fierce headache, and Dallas was strangely silent. The mules didn't like it, either.'

I knew the mountains she meant, from old accounts and maps (obviously I'd never been there). Compared with the Kush to the south and the Himalayas to the east they were pinpricks. But tall enough to have snow at the summit; and hard going for somebody unused to it.

'I saw strange things at the top,' Chillingworth said.

'What kinds of strange things?'

'Aurorae, I guess. Big blocks, I mean like concrete blocks, maybe: seven or eight metres long, three or four wide, one or two thick, and just hurling about in the sky. White noise, and white noise leaching into the air so that I thought it was a blizzard – but then you'd look back where you'd just come from, and the way was clean and sunlit and the air was sharp but still. I said to myself: *be logical, May.* For without logic, what is there? But I failed to integrate my sense data into a coherent system of comprehension.'

'Pretty vivid hallucinations. Sounds like.'

'I thought so, I assumed so. Of course I thought so, I assumed so at the time I thought so. But it wasn't. That wasn't. You see. The blocks, a mustardy-grey colour, were sort of swirling up and over, and then swarming down. Like birds. There were a great many of them. Not all of them were in motion; the closer to the ground they came, the slower, differing speeds one to the other but slower. There was a place, in the pass, where several of them were just there, motionless, suspended a few feet above the ground –in all sorts of orientations with respect to the path. I don't know. I don't know. We examined them, and they sure felt like stone, only warmer than the rocks of the mountains. Approximately smooth to the touch. Sharkskin, maybe. And then one trembled, and swung up and the next thing it was dancing away like a leaf in an autumn gust. Up and through, chaotic pattern, and then eventually to come down again, I don't know. It caught Dallas's mule on its knee, it did, as it swung up, and the beast wailed and ran, and there was blood. I didn't hallucinate the blood. I touched it with fingers and it was wet and sticky to the touch.'

'Strange.'

'And then we were on a downward path, and came below the snowline, and into a valley. Dallas' mule was limping pretty bad, and its coat was all sticky-tar on that leg. But we hadn't come with a medical tricorder, so there wasn't anything we could do. The logical thing would probably have been to put the creature out of its misery and maybe use Dallas's big blade to butcher it and eat it – for although my people are vegetarian, we will eat meat in an emergency, you see. But Dallas grew fierce at the mere suggestion, and so we trudged on.

'We passed the shell of an old tank, half dug into the hillside, the metal of its gun-barrel ripped and ribboned like tinfoil, and the whole of the front covered with rough-textured marmite-coloured rust. It looked like a coat of fur. Relic of the last century. A little further were some old houses, roofless, mudbrick and adobe. Then a bright aluminium hanger; corrugated panels a little speckled with age and the padlocks holding the doors shut rusted into solid brown fists, but shining in the sunlight still. Graffiti painted roughly on the northward wall, some words in Arabic and some in Cyrillic.

'Further down the mules found some grass to eat. Then there was a pebbly descent to a river, and Dallas' mule did something horrible to its ankle on the pebbles. Such an unlucky beast. It brayed and brayed, and a dismounted Dallas looked glum. "It cannot go ahead," he said, and swore in his native tongue.

'So he retrieved his sidearm from the luggage, and aimed it at the creature's head. He held it, like that arm's length; and the moment stretched – the gushing of the river, like the sound of distant applause, the bright sunlight, the fragrant breeze, the wheezing of the wounded mule. Trees shifting uncomfortably in the wind, for all the world as if they were embarrassed.

'Then the mule stopped wailing, and put its heavy head up and heehawed three or four times. I tell you now, my friend, there is no shame in saying that I never learnt Dallas' language – his homeworld language, I mean. We all rely on the universal translator nowadays, don't we?'

'Do we?' I said.

She shook her head. 'I remember now,' she rasped. 'We *did* debate whether it was appropriate to gift your United Nations with the translator technology. But until you discover Warp Drive for yourself, then it was decreed to leave you. Prime directive, you know.'

'Of course,' I said, wondering where the doctor was. 'We quite understand.'

The kitbag lay on the tabletop. I had no desire to look inside, but I supposed I would have to at some point.

'At any rate, after the mule chucked out its raucous noise, Dallas became very agitated. He dropped the gun to the ground – crazy, no? Dropping it might have caused it to discharge accidentally, and one of us might have been shot!'

'Did it?'

'No. Still, I rebuked him. He was trembling, and backing away from the beast. "What is the matter?" I demanded. "What is wrong?"

'"You heard it?" he said. And when I said I heard only

braying, Dallas said, "It spoke my language. It talked to me." Oh I was dubious; of course. It is not logical that a dumb beast should become loquacious, of a sudden, however strange the zone might be. It is not recorded anywhere that such things have happened.'

'Nothing much *is* recorded, though,' I pointed out.

'Logic suggests Dallas was mistaken. But he was shaking as though he had a fever. I said: "What is it? What did the ass say to you?" And he: "Clear as day, in my father-tongue, the language of my homeworld, it said *What have I done unto thee, that thou wouldst smite me with this firearm?*" "Pretty strange thing to say," I said, but Dallas had his back to the steeper side of the gully now, and the mule had limped down to the river and was drinking. "You don't recognise the words?" he yelled at me. "You never read the Bible?" "I have of course heard about this work, an anthology of ancient human holy writing," I said, and I confess I spoke with the disdain that was not wholly logical. "I am of course aware of it, though I have never studied it." "*You* weren't raised with thrice-weekly visits to the South Peckham Pentecostal Chapel," Dallas snarled at me. "Of course not," I told him. "And neither were you – you were raised on Kronos." I had to repeat this last truth three or four times before it sank in, and something of the madness departed from Dallas' eyes. "Only outsiders call it that," he growled at me, and I knew he was back with me. "We native-born have a different word, not fit for the unclean ears of the galaxy's weakling-species."

'We both went down to the river and washed and found some shade and drank bottled water and ate some of our supplies. The hale mule we tied to a tree, and the injured mule, no longer inclined to speech, limped mournfully amongst the stones of the riverbank. Dallas kept looking about, as if he expected to see someone, or something.

"'I consider it unlikely, and therefore illogical, that the human holy Bible would mention firearms," I told him. "It is hard," he replied, and then fell to chewing or mumbling his words. Then he tried again. "It is hard to translate the human Bible's concepts into my language. All that peace and forgiveness: weakness, despicable weakness, so far as we are concerned. Simple as that. There is nothing holy about weakness." "And what is weaker than a crippled mule?" I asked. Dallas scowled at me, and his eyes filled with water – with rage, I suppose, since one of his heritage would surely not burst into tears at such a trivial provocation.

'He wandered into the scrub, and communed with himself for a quarter hour or so. When he came back to me, he was no longer weeping, and was more like his old self. "We cannot proceed with the injured mule. Therefore we must redistribute the baggage. The good mule must carry a great deal, which means you cannot ride. We must walk alongside the mule, and shoulder some of the weight ourselves. As I am stronger, I shall carry more. The greater the glory to me!" I sought to correct him: "My homeworld has a significantly higher gravity than Earth's. Therefore my strength is perfectly competent to the task." But he was in a quarrelsome mood – I mean, even for one of his race. "If your planet truly had a higher gravity your species would have evolved to be squat and muscular, not tall and lean as *you* are." This was a deliberate insult, and I may have said some things in reply which, though of course truthful – since my kind cannot lie – were perhaps not diplomatic. I did not use precisely the word *cowardice*, although it may have been implied. In a fury Dallas took up his firearm again and walked over to the mule.'

'And shot it?'

'No. It turns out, and neither of us had realised it, but the gun was fitted with a chip – handguns all are, nowadays, I suppose. At any rate, the chip had malfunctioned in the zone and the weapon would not fire, not into the donkey's head, not into the air. It was uscless.'

'He had his blade,' I pointed out.

'A savage way to kill a mule,' Chillingworth said. 'In the end we left the creature by the water.'

I was going to say *to die a slow and painful death? Wasn't that rather cruel?* But I thought better of it.

Chillingworth took a breath, tried to breathe it out and started coughing again. This went on for a while, and the colour of her face went from a kind of pale-yellow to a sort of red-gold. Eventually she got the hacking under control, and took another sip of water.

'We went on,' she rasped, 'with one beast, and it was hard walking in the heat of the day, and then easier in the cooler evening. Then we set up tents, one each, and we slept, and before I went to sleep I felt two emotions.'

'Emotions?' I said.

She looked sad, her head shaking from left to right, back and forth as if with a Parkinsonian tremor. 'I know. It is shaming. But I am committed to the truth, to the truth always. And the truth is, I felt two distinct emotional reactions. One was a form of elation – something which my people do not entirely disdain. It is the proper reaction, for instance, to solving a difficult mathematical problem, or resolving some logical paradox. In this case I felt elation that …. Elation that …'

'That you were still alive.'

'Whatever you may have thought when you talked to us, before our journey, we were not fools. We knew the risks, and how likely it was that our journey would end almost as soon as it began, in death. Yet here we were! Still alive. And then I felt a more complicated, and a more shaming emotion. I do not believe that you Earth people have a word for it.'

'A lot of our emotions are like that.'

'I felt a sense of fear, mixed with a kind of horror of passivity that in turn was blended, somehow, with hope. You see, for my people it is very clear: there is truth, and there is error. There is nothing in between. And yet this emotion I experienced was located somewhere in-between. It was the intuition, I suppose, that we had been spared by the Zone because we were not human – that something, or someone, had recognised us as kindred. And that to remain alive we had to be – how can I say this? We had to be careful about falling back into habits of thought that might bring South Peckham Pentecostal Churches into our minds. Do you see what I mean?'

'You had to believe you *were* what you were pre—,' I was going to say *pretending*, but that seemed impolitic, 'what you were presenting yourself to the Zone as.'

She nodded, slowly. 'When Dallas woke me before dawn with shouting and grunting, I first came to consciousness in fear, and then – when I heard that he was barking his native tongue – in relief. I came out of the tent and saw him dancing and swinging his big blade at empty air. The eastern sky was dark but infused with the promise of light: it was just bright enough to see. "Dach'las!" I called out. "What are you doing?" He had shredded his tent, and was whirling like a gyroscope, stabbing and slashing the air. "Angels or Devils," he howled. "All about me!" I looked, but did not see anything, at first, I mean.

'There was nothing I could do – to go closer would be to invite him to slice me with his blade. I assembled our little camping stove and tried to light the flame, though the sparker wouldn't spark. So I rubbed one of our six matchsticks against its abraser and lit the stove that way. Then I made myself coffee, and drank it watching my friend dance about. After a while he wore himself out, or else the visions he was fighting departed. The sun came up, sending streamers of light through the sky like whizzbangs and there were haloes, not one but many stacked haloes, around the head of Dallas.

'Eventually he calmed down, and the haloes thinned and departed. "What did you see?" I asked him. "Was it *them*? We must not assault them, but must instead make overtures. We are diplomats, not invaders." He scowled and muttered something, but his exercise had made him hungry, so he devoured two helpings of supplies and drank a whole bottle of water. When I pointed out to him that it was not logical to consume all our supplies at once, he swore at me in his native language.

"'Logic is of no use in this place," he told me. "This is a place of passion, not logic. This is a place of anger." "I have not found it so," I replied.

"'It is a killing place," he said. "It has killed thousands."

"'Not so many," I said. "Not nearly."

"'But it kills!" It was like he was pouncing on me. "They kill!"

"'They haven't killed us," I pointed out.

"'Because they have recognised in me a worthy opponent – at last," Dallas boomed, standing up and shaking his blade over his head. "They are letting me live so they can fight me! But they have underestimated me!"

"Fascinating," I told him. "But illogical. They have not killed me either, and presumably do not regard me as a warrior."

"'Perhaps they consider you my squire," he laughed.

"'Logic suggests otherwise," I said. And when he laughed in his face – actually came over to me, and levelled his big face next to mine and laughed, such that spittle landed on my cheeks – he repeated: "logic has no place here. This place is not logical."

"'The realm of illogic is *precisely* the place for logic," I said. "It is crying out for the healing touch of logic! I reason that once we have solved the dynamic of this place, understood it according to the protocols of logic, then *they* will reveal themselves to us." "And then I can fight them in single combat!" he said. "No, no, that is not the reason we came to this place. My friend, have you forgotten? We shall bring about a new age for the people of the Earth!" At this he said something that made me afraid.'

'What?' I asked.

'He said: "What care I for Earth? What do either of us care

for these primitive people? Something grander is happening, and it does not concern them." I realised then that he was – how can I say this without it sounding offensive? – reverting to a more primitive version of his species. He was no longer the kind-hearted, attentive, dedicated guy I had known for fifteen years... the Federation version of Dallas, you might say. He was now Dah'las, ancient warrior of an alien world.'

'Wasn't it better for you both that...' I started to say. But I couldn't think of a diplomatic way of saying *that he was committing so convincingly to the play-acting,* so I said nothing.

I looked again at the kit-bag on the table.

'There was no point in sitting around,' Chillingworth said, in a thin, wheezy voice. 'We packed up and continued down the valley, letting the mule drink from time to time. We came to a deserted village: some roofless houses with horizontal and vertical icicles of broken glass in the window frames. We looked into a few but there was nothing much inside. Faded children's toys, torn rugs, books whose pages melted to crumbs and ashes when we opened them. We found an abandoned false leg in one of the houses: an old-style articulated prosthesis with a shoe on its wooden foot.

'The valley turned left, and we climbed a shallow slope dotted with acacia trees. An empty village, dotted with poplar trees, was silent, Butterflies twitched through the sunlight. Most of the houses here were mud-walled, and several still had their roofs. I looked inside one, and the ceiling was a seething mass of spiders, fat as apples, skin like weather-stained grey leather. We left that place well alone.

'Over the next hill and we found a large field filled with what looked like the broken off stubs of black and khaki columns. They were metal, and somebody had gone to the bother of arranging them in rows. Unexploded bombs, undetonated shells – thousand-pound bombs fat as barrels, thin torpedo-like shells, at the far end of the field slim shells like courgettes – all stuck in the soil as if somebody madly expected them to sprout to life. Some of them had faded Cyrillic letters on their side; some had English characters. "Maybe a graveyard?" Dallas said to me. "Perhaps warriors are buried here, and marked with these weapons." "Possible," I said. "But unlikely." I didn't like this field, I did not like its atmosphere. You Earth people say "vibe". I distrusted this vibe. We passed on. Over the brow of the hill we stepped over a low tumbledown wall and found a field full of polyhedra. Deep blue, irridescing faintly with a kind of algae-green and a maple-syrup yellow gold.'

'Polyhedra?' I said, wondering if I had heard correctly.

'Some were as big as a car. Some were small as those dice tabletop gamers use. Some had seven sides, some eleven, some even had thirteen and seventeen.'

'I don't understand. Was there writing on any of these poly, er, hedrons?'

'Not that we could see. I wondered if whoever had arranged all the old shells on the other side of that hill – the old missiles from various historical Afghan wars – I wondered if they were in some way imitating these... shapes. But the shells were all in symmetrical rows. These were disposed into no pattern that I could see. Scattered about. Some gleamed with light when touched. Others were inert. And there were odder aspects: the smaller ones were just as heavy as the bigger ones.'

'How heavy are you talking?'

'More than a man. Less than a car. I don't know. It was strange. Dallas was keen to carry one away as a souvenir, so he chose one of the small ones and heaved it, grunting and swearing, up. This he placed in his pocket, but it only ripped through the fabric and bruised his leg as it tumbled again to the floor. He blamed me for that.'

'Why?'

'Oh, there was no logic in the blame. But isn't that the way with anger? At any rate, we walked on.

'Eventually twilight came, attended by a great many insects, and we pitched our one remaining tent. We used a second match and lit a fire, against the cold of the Afghan night. Dallas grew confidential – though I had known him fifteen years, and attended many cons and events with him, he told me things that night I did not know about him. I am not sure if it would be appropriate for me to reveal to *you* what he said. It might be a breach of confidence.'

'I understand your scruple,' I said.

'One thing, conceivably, *is* relevant. He told me he had been in love only once, and with a human girl. But he was worried that he would hurt her – I asked "emotionally, you mean?" and perhaps there was disdain in my voice. For emotions are a kind of pathology. But he said, "She was small and beautiful and fragile, and I'm a big lunk. A big brute." Then he told me a story about the genitals of his kind, which are smooth when sex is only for recreation, but when it is for procreation they develop spines along the length of the shaft. "That sounds very painful," I told him. "We aim to create a warrior in the act of sex," he growled, "and my culture believes that a warrior is conceived as he is born – in blood." I confess I had never heard this story before, and I consider myself a true-fan, well versed in all the ins-and-outs of all the different varieties of alien and human life. Besides, it struck me as illogical, and I told Dallas so. "Surely causing tissue trauma in such an intimate place would act against the chance of the fertilised egg successfully implanting?" "Maybe in a human female," he grumbled. And then he began weeping again, the second time had done so during our time in the Zone.

'There was a bright moon out, as round and white as a starship hull. And the fire radiated a great deal of light. There was no mistaking what he was doing. At first his weeping only embarrassed me. He kept saying this human girl's name, over and over, and telling the night sky how sorry he was. And crying!

And this, you understand, was not true to his species.'

'Oh,' I said.

'At first I thought there were insects, but the swarm grew very quickly and very dense, and the moon was no longer visible. I grew frightened that we had violated the terms of our passage into the zone, and leapt to my feet. All I could do was slap Dallas, and try to rouse him to anger, but to begin with he was too miserable to react. I called out the few words of his language I had in my memory, and then found a stick and cracked it across his back. Finally he did grow angry, and picked up his blade and threatened me; and I felt the panic recede within me, and the rule of reason and logic resume.'

'What about the swarm? *Was* it insects?'

'The swarm drew back from us, and I do not believe it was insects. Whatever it was, it had killed our mule, and so we were in a pickle. We squeezed into the one tent, and slept badly, and when the dawn came we sorted through our luggage and reduced it to two carry-able backpacks, and then walked on. When the sun was in the zenith we rested in the speckled shade of some poplars, and Dallas slept. I did not, for I saw movement through the trees, and went off to investigate.'

'Movement? I asked. 'What – animals?'

'I thought I saw people. I believed I had seen three people, and they were all wearing bright yellow hijabs, which surprised me because I thought hijabs were always black. They were carrying pots, one per person, and were making their way down a path towards a lake. But I was tired, and woozy, and I think I imagined it. At any rate there were no people by the lake, although there were some wild chickens.'

'So you didn't see any people in the Zone?'

'Not living. We saw corpses. Many corpses. Many. Madness has no purpose. Or reason. But it may have a goal. There were people mummified by light and heat and wind. There were people whose arms ended in poked-out bones as if they had drawn back their flesh as a man rolls up his sleeves. There were many heads. Many heads in heaps and pyramids'

I looked at the kit-bag, lying unopened on the table.

'Pyramids of, what? Skulls?'

She shook her head, with a precise motion. 'There were some birds, but very few, and none flew close enough for me to see if they were biological creatures or – something else. We saw no foxes or jackals. The insects were, I believe, all miniature drones. Logically, there was a paucity of animals who might devour the flesh of the dead. It would decay in time, I suppose; but the actions of the climate tended to mummify it.'

'I don't understand.'

'A head cannot be a skull if it still has flesh upon its bones.'

'Oh,' I said, understanding.

'Once I saw a machine, very large, many miles distant. It was shaped like a letter, but one of prodigious size. Perhaps a hundred metres long.'

'Shaped like a letter? You mean an alphabetic letter? Which one?'

'I did not recognise the letter,' she said. And then, immediately, 'Oh, I do not mean an English letter. A Hebrew letter, I think, with many spars. Or a hieroglyph. It had legs, and so far as I could see from my distant vantage, there were wheels, or caterpillar tracks, on the end of its legs. It had five legs, I think, and swung them round, and made a slow ungainly progress across the landscape. It passed behind a hill and I could no longer see it.'

'How big did you say?'

'It is hard to gauge. Longer than a passenger plane, I think.'

'I have to tell you – the whole area is continually monitored. Nobody has seen any gigantic machines.'

She nodded, again with a weird, automata-like precision. 'I understand. There are several possible explanations. For example it might be cloaked in such a way as only to be visible from ground-level. All U.N. surveillance is from high altitudes, I believe.'

'That's true.'

'Another possibility is that we had been transported into some other realm, far from human perception. Perhaps a real world, perhaps a simulation. I suggested this to Dallas, and he grew wrathful. "This is not simulation!" he boomed. "I know the dream from the real life!"'

'Was this before or after you saw the giant, er, moving structure?'

'After. We had spent an uncomfortable night, and we were having breakfast. Dallas was in a poor mood. "Has your so-called logic solved this place, then? Can you explain it?" I told him it was not a matter of explanation, but of theories that fitted the observable facts, better or worse. He mocked this. "Reason is thin, but courage and strength are not," he said.

'"In what way does your courage explain this place?" I asked him. I confess I was growing angry.

'"We have died, and gone to hell – the hell of my people, where we will eventually confront Fek'lhr, the Satan of my people," he roared. "And when we do I shall fight him!"

'"Be serious," I said. "We both know there is no magic or religion at work here. This is the technology of an alien civilisation. Perhaps it is a holographic simulation. Perhaps passing over the mountains, where we saw the giant blocks flying through the air, was some kind of transporter beam, and we have been taken to some other location, perhaps some other world."

'"That is what logic tells you?" he scoffed. But I could see he was intrigued at the idea.

'"Perhaps," I said, "the transportation has been not through space but time. Consider the field with the strange polydhera. Consider the insects: might they not be future technology? Maybe the Zone is sparing us not because we are dressed as aliens, but because we are dressed as beings from the future. Maybe the Zone is a time travel artefact, a consequence of something, or some people, in the future…"

"'People?" he said, sharp-like. "You mean, *not* aliens?"

A wind burlied down the slope and made the surface of the river shiver as though it was afraid. The acacias hissed.

"'If humans, then advanced humans," I said, hurriedly. "From an advanced civilisation capable of time travel." But I confess I was growing nervous. There were swarms in the sky, away to the north. The quality of the light had become strange. This talk of non-aliens, of,' she swallowed, 'of, talk of humans, was making me nervous. As for Dallas, well. It only made him angry. "*Cowards* from the future," he snarled. "Hiding. Why won't they face me?"

"'Whoever *they* are, violence is surely not the best frame of mind in which to encounter *them*," I said. I believe I spoke reasonably! Do you not think so? But Dallas would have none of this. He grew furious, and began tearing branches from a nearby acacia.

"'I've seen all the surveillance footage – a wasteland, of course. The whole place! What are we even doing here?"

"'*You* ask that?" I said, astonished at him. Really he was not like himself. He yelled something in his native language. "You were the one who wished to come," I reminded him. "You insisted upon it, in fact. I wasn't even booked-in for this trip, my friend!"

"'You said we would meet them!" he roared. "So where are they?"

"'Let us go and find them, then," I said. So we packed up and explored, but everywhere was the same: a wasteland. Weeds and dirt. The wind in the leaves. A small waterfall pissing into a pool. An old tarpaulin impaled on the many branches of a tree. A mass of red-black rust heaped into the shape of a car's chassis.

The swarm of insects followed us, at a distance. From time

to time Dallas would stop and wave his blade at the swarm, and shout at it in his own language. As the sun set the swarm settled into the long grass two hundred metres away from us. Neither of us wanted to investigate.

'That night we slept in the dark, with strange buzzings swirling around and above our cramped little shared tent. The next day there was a strange smell on the breeze, and we loitered, and Dallas practised dead-heading weeds with his blade. But that night the sun seemed not to set, and the whole land gleamed with light – every mountain shining with a pallor like moonlight, but all combined together to make for a neon world. And the land itself shifted – the landscape, I mean. Geometric forms, pushing up from below. We had made our tent on a slope that led down to the river, the easier to fetch water and wash and so on, and on the far side of the stream the land rose again. I sat and watched this ground crumble and reassemble into hexagons, each one three metres across – like the Giant's Causeway, do you know it?'

'I know it.'

'And the following morning, one of the mountains had shucked off its geological rough edges and imperfections and had become as pure a pyramid as if the Egyptians had built it. I suggested to Dallas that we walk to that place, though I conceded it was very far way. The mere suggestion made him very angry indeed.'

'Angry?' I looked, once again with unease, at the unopened kitbag on the table.

'He said, "Woman, no". This was not his normal manner of addressing me, and I considered it disrespectful, and told him so. He said, "Woman, you have brought me to a land without honour.'

'"So you wish to return, is that it?" I said. "Empty-handed, back to the mundane world?"

'"Woman," he said, and his eyes shone. There were elements

within his eyes and they shone out golden-brown. "Where are you *from*?" There was ferocity in him as he spoke.

"'The planet Vulcan," I told him. "As you know very well!'"

"'Cheltingham," he barked. "Cheltinghaaam Ladies College."

"'Don't be absurd!' I retorted, although I confess I was feeling scared now. "There is no such place on my homeworld with any such name –'"

"'But you used to say you were half *yooman*, yeah? What was it, yooman mummy? Yooman daddy?'"

"'Dah'las –' I tried, but he raised his blade and advanced on me. "Don't make me nerve-pinch you," I screamed. I was very afraid. Then, pleading: "Dallas. Stop. We're friends, remember?"

"'*My* kind – friends with *your* kind?" he retorted, sounding a little more like himself. "Pass the time of day, and that. But friends? Cheltingham *Ladies* College, and daddy's little trust fund, was it? And you know where I grew up?"

"'You grew up as the scion of a great warrior's family on Kronos." But I could feel the sense of things starting to slip out of true. It was not a comfortable sensation. It was not –'

Chillingworth stopped, breathing noisily. She said, 'It was the fraying, of...' but her voice sounded like a kazoo. She coughed, and coughed, and finally spat out a chunk of something onto the tabletop, where it lay, glistening like eggwhite. 'I told him, "Don't be a fool, Dallas. It'll get us both – it's not just you. We are each supporting one *another* in this place".'

"'And me?" he bellowed, and he swung his blade through the air. "Dulwich? Dulwich my arse. Called it Dulwich on the signage, but it was Peckham, and a big borg-blocky stack of ex-council flats, with a distant view of Nunhead cemetey." His native language was deserting him. I could hear it! Ex-Cansel. Nunedd. And though I shouted at him, "Kronos! Kronos! You grew up on Kronos!" the demons were on him then – even I could see them, and to him they were as real as the air he was breathing, and they *were* as real, too. "Three times a week!" he bellowed, as he cut at the flying creatures singing about his head as he danced back and forth. "Peckham Pentecostals, and my Mum could 'it me with her own air-dryer if I so much as scowled, right in the face. Week in week out." We were attacked.'

'Attacked?' I repeated

'It came out of the ground – like a dragon-worm, though smaller, I suppose. Big as an anaconda, but once it shook off the dirt and was airborne, its skin gleamed like oiled peacocks, and it had so many teeth they were spilling out of its maw and dotting the whole skull, and it riled out of the dust and reared up over us both. But it was Dallas the beast was after. It took him then. Oh, he roared, he roared, and I screamed, I daresay, though there's no logic in such a reaction. And when I thought everything was lost I heard him bellow once again in his native tongue, in his warrior's language, and the blade spiked through the back of the beast in a spurt of purple gore, and then he was slashing and slashing and the monster fell apart like a piñata full of butcher's leavings, red gobbets and yellow membrane.'

'He killed the beast? It was – an organic creature?'

'He was standing there, panting. The demons were retreating, and as I looked up they looked like nothing so much as a flaw in the purity of the sky's-blue, like a kink in reality. But reason told me that the whole zone was such a place, and the kink had purpose, and the purpose was – I think it was puzzled by us. Maybe it wasn't quite certain whether it could see us. Or –'

She stopped. Motionless.

'Go on,' I prompted.

Nothing. It was as if a robot had had its switch flicked off. I moved a little closer. 'Are you all right?'

She looked at me, and for the first time I could see that there was something not right about her eyes. There was an intricate pattern of lines, a sort of radial grid, linking irises and whites.

I really didn't know what to make of this.

I waited.

'All right,' she said, eventually.

'It feels foolish calling you *Chillingworth*,' I told her, putting a hand on her shoulder. 'What's your first name?'

'Mabel,' she said.

'And Dallas? What was his first name?'

'Dallas was his first name.'

'Mabel,' I said, gently. 'Can you see me? Are you blind?'

'He wept,' she said. 'After that. You have to understand, the beast he had fought was still there, its remains, its butchered body parts. It stank – I could smell it: an oily, acetone sort of smell, decay and poison mixed with – I don't know. Chemically stench. It was no hallucination, for he had seen it and I had seen it, and he had cut it to pieces with his blade. Then he stood over me, and sticky shreds of the creature were still sticking to him, draped over his clothing. But why wouldn't all that please a warrior? Except that then he threw his blade away and sat down beside me, and started to weep. This was the third time he had wept. In that place.'

I tried to picture the big feller I had met crying. Not easy. 'What was it?'

'He said to me, "When I became a fan" and then he couldn't speak any more, because he was wailing like a babby. Like a babby.' Chillingworth looked around herself with her weird eyes; was she seeing the environment, or something else superimposed upon it? Or *was* she blind?

'Go on,' I urged, again. 'Fan? Yes?'

'I knew what he was saying,' she replied. 'Because I felt the same way. For him, it was all tangled up with his family life, with being brought up super-religious, his whole community – his world – super-religious. Peace and love and forgiveness, but policed with the sharp tongues of mothers and aunts, and smacks on the head, and mind games and threats and all the weight of the monstrous afterlife pressing down upon him. He realised from an early age, it *was* war. It was all war, God and Satan, family and individuality, his mother's will against his. And he realised that he wanted war. But he wanted a *clean* war. He wanted it to be about bravery and strength, not cunning and shame and psychological pressure and guilt and…' She stopped to try and get her breath back. 'And all that.'

'He told you all this?'

'I knew him fifteen years. We were friends. He told me a lot. And I know that he floundered, caught in the net, until he discovered Fandom. And there it was! A new community – a new tribe. A new set of beliefs, not about purity and the ten commandments and hate-yourself, but about a federation of inclusiveness. About a future without money and racism and religion, clean and rational and freeing. In his old life, Dallas had to conform. In his new community he could dress up, to *play*. And he played at his inner truth, which was that he was an honourable man and a warrior and that became his outer truth as well. And then the Zone –'

She was wheezing more now. She paused to scrape together enough breath to continue.

'The Zone meant that play had to become serious. Had to become work. But then he and I thought we could leverage our passion into something bigger – first contact! Fame for us, fortune maybe. But validation, you know? Validation. All the sneering and the snideness rebutted. So we came here, and Dallas became the warrior he had always wanted to be. He was…' She broke off.

'You keep talking about him in the past tense,' I pointed out.

'At one point I had to remind him: "We came here to make contact," I said. "And to take *their* message back to the world.

Don't lose sight of the mission, Dallas!" And he was scornful. "Why should they be any different?" he said. "Think you've escaped class, and then you discover it's been in your face the whole time. You think *they* don't prize aristocracy and despise the poor? Look where we are. You know what Afghanistan was before the Zone." he said. "It was one of the poorest countries in the world, that's what. It was the prole of the international community. What chance did it ever have? What chance did I ever have?"'

'I don't follow,' I said.

'It was the same for me,' she wheezed. 'I was cleverer than my...' and she stopped. 'All the hysterics and the gin and the family drama. Drama dignifies it: hysteria, rather. But logic was the...' and she stopped again. She peered at me with her weird eyes.

'*Can* you see me, Mabel?'

'We always have logic,' she said. 'Logic and reason and self-control, self-control. Self-control is other-control, but the more crucial thing is. So, at any rate, I got away. I found something else. And friends. These were my people. And then the Zone happened, and it was clear to us that others, that extra-terrestrial. That. That extrasolar others had created it. That reinforced our sense that we knew the truth. Angels and devils – pff. Of course,' she added, a strange thrum in her voice, 'I know the truth about the Zone now because I've *been* there.'

I left it for a moment, but when she didn't say anything else, I prompted: 'What is the truth of the Zone, Mabel?'

But she was coughing now, not speaking, and there was something different about the noise she was making, a harsher car-engine rattle. She pushed her chair back and put her head on her knees, her whole body shuddered and she coughed, coughed, coughed. I didn't know what to do. She was changing colour.

'I'll get you some water,' I said.

I stood up, and at that moment heard the sound of an incoming shell. It was a most startling thing, because it brought me back to where I was. Where I had always been. And, a little way to the west, came the crunch of impact, and the shudder that passed through the whole building and made the windows rattle in their frames like packed wineglasses in a shaken box. Dust drifted down from the ceiling. Outside the sound of a car alarm, like a seagull – and how long since I had heard a seagull? Many years. I went to the window, and looked out. Pre-dawn light gleamed in the eastern sky. We'd been up all night. I hadn't realised that the time had gone by so quickly. From my vantage I could see through the grey: two kinked and puffy pillars of black smoke about a third of a mile away, which meant there had been two impacts. Why hadn't I heard the first?

I went across the hall and into the office and from there I called again on the city-grid landline – engaged, engaged, and then somebody was there. 'I need a doctor,' I said. 'I have somebody at the UN Mission, and she's really pretty poorly. I called hours ago and nobody has come.'

'We'll get to you when we get to you,' said the person on the other end. An accent, Scandinavian, perhaps, or German. 'There have been three blasts, and we're undertaking triage.'

Three? Why had I only heard one? 'Where's the shelling coming from?'

'We're not sure. Seems that it might be from the Zone, but of course that is impossible. So perhaps it's from China? Long-range?'

'Christ,' I said. 'But why?'

'Why? Who asks that question *here*?'

'Please – I have a person here, Mabel Chillingworth, she has been into the Zone and come out again alive. It's imperative we don't let her die. For her own sake, of course, but also for what she could teach us about the Zone.'

'That sounds a pretty tall story,' said the person at the other end, and hung up.

I fetched a glass of water and got back to Mabel. She was trembling and doubled-over, but the coughing has stopped. She took a sip, took another, and then she slid off the chair onto the floor in a faint.

I am not a particularly strong person, but Mabel, though tall, was very thin, so I was able to lift her and get her up the stairs to a bed on the first floor. Here she lay on her back and moaned. I took a look at her hands. The space between her ring finger and her middle-finger had, on both hands, been opened up, a gash reaching right down, almost to the wrist. The same thing had happened to the gap between thumb and index. The flesh of the wounds was not open, or even scabbed; it was covered with skin. The lines of her palm curved round into the gap. It looked like an old wound, very old and part-healed. The fingers themselves were twisted, corkscrewed and kinked and all but the middle finger on the left hand had no fingernails left on them. They looked very odd.

Her ears were black and rusted with old blood scabs. It looked as though tiny claws had ripped at them over and over.

There was another high-pitched whistle, and I flinched, waiting for the impact; but it passed over head and the crump, when it came, was a long way to the south. The house barely shook.

Medicine, I thought. I didn't know what, but it seemed a better bet than just sitting helplessly and waiting. I brought the red box – no white cross on its lid, of course, in this country – from the bathroom and rummaged inside. There didn't seem anything very relevant to her circumstances. Should I bandage her ears? Administer a pain killer?

I went downstairs and rang a person I knew in the Defence Force, to see if there was any news on where the shelling was coming from. Nobody seemed to know anything. So then I went back up again. Mabel was awake.

'Are you all right? Are you feeling any better?'

'Hunky,' she rasped, 'and dory.'

'Mabel,' I said. 'What happened to Dallas?'

She was lying on her back and staring, I suppose – though I never got to the bottom of what she saw with those strange, grid-overlaid eyeballs – at the ceiling. For a while she said nothing, and then she said, 'I held him when he wept. We'd been friends for fifteen years. If I were ever to fall for a man it would have been him. When he'd finished crying of course he felt angry with himself. Felt demeaned. That made him cruel. And cruel to me. Before that, though, he was crying like a child and saying, "I've brought you to this, pal," says he. "Brought you out of your happy life to die in Kafiristan." Which was only half true, since I examined the prospect logically and determined it was worth the risk, and elected to come of my own free will. When his face was still wet he said, "Say you forgive me, May." "I do," I told him. "Fully and freely do I forgive you, my friend." But the forgiveness, maybe, made him think of his childhood, and the Peckham chapel, and that only pepped up his anger again. So he stopped weeping and wailing and broke off from me. Then he stood up and looked all about him, and put his head back and looked into the sky. Storm clouds were in the middest of the blue, now, only they weren't clouds filled with rain, they were swarms of – I don't know what they were, I still don't know. Insects, maybe. Demons, maybe. Nanobots and miniaturised drones from some future war, manufactured by the million whose interacting perceptions and ordnance had shaken reality free of its baseline, here, here, now, in Kafiristan.'

'Drones?' I pressed. 'Like – miniaturised drones? Mabel, is *that* what you saw?'

'And I tried to reason with him. "Your wrath is not logical," I said. "Consider the facts and banish emotion from you. Other people have come into this zone and all died. We have survived, at least this far, and there must be a logical reason as to why." "Hang logic," he bellowed and took up his blade. "War is not

logical." And that was a puzzler, it truly was, because of course
he was right. Diplomacy is logic, and negotiation is logic, and
mutual interest and rational discussion are all logic. But war is
when logic breaks down. "Why here?" he kept shouting. "You
know why it is here of all places? It was war when Alexander the
Great marched up on his velociraptor mounts. It was war when
the Mughul emperor came with a million men. It was war when
the British rode in, Victorians with machine guns, and tried to
conquer, and then the Russians, and then the Taliban fighting
everyone, and then the Americans, and now – me! It's always
been war. And you'll say, Europe was always war too, why didn't
the Zone come there? Or Israel, or some Central African
republic where they're always oiling their antique AKs. And I'll
say that in those places you have war and peace, and in this place
only war. It's in the midpoint between Europe and the Far East,
because Moscow and Mumbai, between the mountains of Tibet
and the flatlands of the Sinai. It's the centre of the world, and
they saw that, and *they* saw that the meaning of that centre is
always war. And that's why *I* am here!"

"Be careful, Dallas," I warned him, for the swarm overhead
was coming closer, and expanding as it sank towards us.

"Shake hands, my logical comrade," says he. "I'll shake your
hand before I slaughter you – fair fight, mind. Fair fight." For
the second time I was scared of him. For the second time. "If
you come any closer I'll have to nerve-pinch you," I told him,
but my voice was all starlings and wobblings and he wasn't
impressed. "You couldn't nerve pinch a three-year-old child,"
he told me, flat. "It's always been play-acting with you, hasn't it?
Public-school drama society," and he said spoke the words
mockingly, *draw, maw*. "Dressing up and what fun what-ho. You
think *we're* aliens? You think we're ET?" He wasn't really
shouting at me, you understand. He was yelling at the sky, and
the swarm came down lower and by goodness and in all badness
it looked mean. It was formed of mechanical locusts, black-

53

bodied future-tech, millions of units. Enough to bring death to the whole world, or that's what I thought then. "Look at us! Look at us! *We're* not aliens," he yelled. "We're not even human beings, because human beings are complex, and we are one note. We are simplified human beings. You are what a human looks like when all the other aspects of humanity are reduced to logic. I am what a human looks like when everything is reduced to anger. I reckon I am closer to a regular human than you are, but we're neither of us *that* close. You think we are? Look at us. We're cartoon humanity, the one dimensional woman and the one dimensional man. You think this Zone thinks we're alien? It didn't kill us because we didn't come up to the standard of regular humanity – it didn't kill us any more than it killed our mules."

"'Those mules," I said, an answering spark of anger coming into me now, "*are* both dead." But he scoffed at that.

'So he launched himself towards me, and logic helped me obtain a kind of clarity, and the clarity reached out to the whole cool bright sky and the whole blocky polyhedral land. Dallas uttered his war cry, and brought his blade up above his shoulders, and I brought all my logical ratiocination to bear on the immediacy of this moment. One particularised moment, in time. The swarm overhead was twenty feet away, and had spread out into a ceiling that muted the sun, and I could hear the humming of their engines, or motors, or whatever it was that kept them airborne. He ran at me, my friend of fifteen years, my fellow Fan, and he kicked me hard. He lifted his heavy leg and kicked me hard, and I took it in the chest. Bruised me, it did, and I went onto my back. He was standing over me. "You know what these alien races really mean?" he said. "You want to know what this cosplay actually says? You in your pale blue and your reason and logic and cool command – you say *middle class*. And me, treating every day as if I'm going to die that day. Me with my rage and no way to express it but fighting, I say *prole*."

""The Federation is a classless society," I gasped, because it hurt to breathe and it hurt more to speak and I was wondering if he'd snipped a chip out of a rib, with his big hulking foot.

""That's literally the most middle-class thing anyone can say!" he bellowed. He really shouted this time. "You can't see it, like a fish can't see water. *Your* captain owns a vineyard in France! Your humanoid android is a professor at Oxford! Your method of flying about the galaxy is to sit in a comfortable armchair in a suburban sitting room, watching the universe through a high-definition widescreen television!"

""It's *us*, Dallas!" I pleaded. "It's not me, it's you and me. We're both fans – you are, just as much as I am! It's where we belong – not as one class and another, but as equals. Not as black and white, but *equals*. Exploring the universe together."

""This show," he yelled. "This show! You think they were taken in by our cosplay, even for a minute?"

""We are still alive," I said. "Therefore logic decrees that we have managed to convince *them* –" I stopped, because I couldn't be sure what we had convinced *them* of.

""We're only alive if we get out of here alive, and we'll neither of us do that. You're going to tell me every scientist who's come in here, every soldier and explorer, since the Zone first appeared – you think they didn't face something just like this? None of them survived, and we won't. You're going to tell me why you think we're not lying there, *not* breathing, in the foothills face down in the dust, just north of Bagram, whilst some UN observer peers at us through binoculars and tuts sadly to himself and goes back to his cup of green tea? And you know what? That don't even bother me, May, because today is a good die to die!" And then he started shouting in his native tongue, the guttural language of that faraway planet, and the whole ceiling of locusts convulsed and lifted itself a metre, or maybe two.

My heart was hammering in my chest. I didn't want to die, I didn't. "You've been a fan for decades, Dal," I said. "Don't tell me you hated it, all this time."

"'Only look what I became, May! I became the Soviet alien – the Native American alien – the Black-man alien – the violent alien with the ugly face. This is who," and he swore, "who – I – am!"

And he lifted his blade. Everything became clear to me, then. My thoughts were sharp as white light.

'That's when the ceiling descended, like a great mass if black hailstones. And when Dallas looked up there was glee in his face, because, well, you know why. Because he was proving his point to *them*, and to me, and to you too. That.'

'So that was when he died?' I glanced again at the unopened kit-bag.

'They took his head. They took his head as he swiped at them with his big blade, and then they were all over them – and me too. Me they crucified, or that was how it felt, stretched me out, my hands pierced, and my feet too, and my own clear-thinking head the centre of the hailstorm.' She stopped. 'He didn't really say those things, I suppose. My friend of fifteen years, my friend... I don't know what he thought. I did not mind-meld with him before he died. I never did such a thing with him. What an invasion of privacy that would have been! Can you imagine what he would have said? *The quintessential bourgeois entitlement, that not even the thoughts and inner-feelings of the proles be hidden from them! The essence of all oppression of the poor, that their privacy be perfectly eliminated!* Well, no, he wouldn't have used language like that, would he. That's the point. Wouldn't you say?'

'Stay with me,' I said. 'The doctors should be here soon. We can take a full statement – you have amazing things to tell the world. Just hold on.'

'I don't know what he thought, as the cloud came down. But I would guess he was happy. He died fighting, and the – and *they* did more than simply stop his heart, or scorch his cerebral cortex, or whatever they did to those earlier explorers. They treated him as he treated them: with knives. He had one, and they had a million, and just for a moment he was plumb in the middle of dizzy dancing ropes of swarming machinery, curling around him. Then it was: cut through the neck, take the head, slice the body into twenty thousand parts, and it took half an hour, or it took a moment. I had my own worries then. The pain was very bad. My people are supposed to have a high threshold for pain. But, isn't it possible that I do indeed have a high pain threshold, but that they exceeded it? Do you see what they did to my hands?' She held her hands out to me. 'And they did the same to my feet, if you take off these old fur boots you'd see. God knows why they did my feet too. And when they were finished – next day, I felt it was, a miracle that I wasn't dead – I had been robbed of all my carefully cultivated composure. I writhed in the dust.

'I saw visions. Dallas came back to me, at the head of an army – an army! Not a human army, mind. Autochthons. Metal. He said, "You know how the holodeck worked? It would create a terrain that moved under your feet, like a gym treadmill, as you walked, and you might trek for weeks through ever changing landscapes and never go anywhere."

'"It's no holodeck," I said, crying tears with the pain in all the limbs of my body. My face wet and my nose gluey with snot and my diaphragm plunging up and down to force odd emphases onto the words.

'"It's no holodeck," Dallas repeated. He was whole again, and his brown skin was glowing, and there was a halo round his head, and I knew in my gut he wasn't real. I didn't know, and I still don't know, if he was my imagination, or if he was *them*, somehow. "Doesn't it make you think of something, though? The holodeck? You don't move, the universe moves around you? The suburban sofa-chair, planted immoveable in front of the television. Eppur si muove!" There was lots of stuff like this, stuff Dallas himself would never have said. "The people's flag is deepest red, but what about those characters clothed in this proletarian colour? They are the quintessentially disposable! What greater enemy than the Borg, and what are they but the nightmare libel on collectivisation and communism? No laws for the ruling classes, the captains, if they decide the prime directive ought to be disregarded then disregarded it is; for them the whole cosmos is a playground – alien women to seduce, alien men to oppress. There is even a machine, the replicator, that can make any product, rendering labour itself worthless and so guaranteeing the endless subaltern denigration of that whole class." There was much more like this.

'I believe I fell asleep, but the pain in my hands and my feet was such that I couldn't sleep for long. Then I saw the sky full of craft – vessels – brick-shaped white-silver craft, and much higher up ankh-shaped craft, lampstands standing on their two splayed legs, white flattened sputniks with swollen trailing antennae, and here and there a green metallic gigantic spermatozoon and the anaconda beast I had seen before, I don't know, but larger than ever, larger than worlds, than stars, a great stiff hollow tube rumbling overhead and sucking up all the other craft, which were, by comparison, insect-sized.

'I sat up and dragged myself over to my backpack and ate some supplies, somehow managed to get them to my mouth. There were some painkillers in there and I took them. If I'd had a walking stick I would have used that, but there was nothing save Dallas's bloodstained and discarded blade; so I wrapped a globe of cloth around the sharp end and plodded away with this makeshift staff. My eye was on the mountains. I could not shoulder my pack, and the sun was out, and I knew I would not last long on the single bottle of water tucked into the back of my pants. But I told myself: *the snow on the mountain tops looks inviting. That's water, isn't it? I can drink it, can't I?*

'I don't remember walking to the mountains. Only – I was there, and the water bottle tucked into my waistband was frozen solid and burning the skin in the small of my back – I have the scar,' and she tried to turn in the bed to show me, but I pressed her shoulder back down and said I believed her. She took a while getting her breath back, and then went on: 'It was a cruel bad country, and the cloth came off the top of Dallas's blade, so I couldn't grasp it except that it would cut my hand. And I'm sorry to say I left it there, for I would have liked to have brought it back. But there was a blizzard, too. Not like the blizzard we experienced on the way in, but a heap of snow flying up in strong wind. But my old friend and fellow fan and bold goer Dallas walked before and said: "Come along, May, my girl. It's a big thing we're doing." The mountains, they danced at night, and the mountains they tried to fall on my logical head, but Dallas he held up his hand, and I came along behind him, though bent double. She never let go of Dallas's hand, that logical girl, and she never let go of Dallas's head, for though I could not bear the weight of my pack I would not leave that small sack behind. It ought to have taken me months to walk that countryside, yet in a twink I was in amongst the snow, and my face went numb and my hair stiffened and broke off; and in another twink I was on the outskirts of Kabul. The sun warmed me then, and the pain was terribly terrible when the feeling came back into my face and hands and feet.'

'You had some kind of assistance, getting out,' I said to her.

'It's all holding us off with one arm and drawing us on with the other. But isn't that the logic of the universe? Maybe I should say tentacle, rather than arm. Maybe I should say metal prong. Jesus, I don't know.'

She shut her eyes, then, and didn't say any more, and I left her alone. She needed to sleep.

I made myself another tea and sat on the terrace in the dawn-light. A sinking exhaustion took hold of me. I dozed, and when I woke, with a jerk, the sun was two hand spans higher in the sky. Alí was at my side. 'Sahib, the doctor is here, the doctor has come.'

Four

I went down, yawning, and shook the doctor's hand, and the two of us went up to where Mabel was. Except that she wasn't there any more. I searched the whole house in a hurry, but she was gone. I apologised to the doctor for calling her out on a wild-goose chase, and described Chillingworth's physical condition so vividly that she insisted we had to locate her and get her medical attention.

Downstairs, her kitbag was on the table; when she had gone she had decided not to take it with her. I was still not ready, yet, to look inside it.

With Alí's help the doctor and I did a quick sweep of the local area, but did not find her. I went to the lodgings she and Dallas had taken in Chicken Street, but there was nobody there. At lunchtime I took a break; Alí fixed me some couscous and fried vegetables, and I discovered I was very hungry. After eating I discovered I was very tired, so I slept for an hour. The ringing of the landline woke me, and I stumbled down to answer it with a gummy mouth.

'We found her,' said the doctor, though the whizzing and creaking of the telephone line. 'But it's not good news. She was wandering bare-headed in the midday sun for hours, and her face is badly sunburned and blistered. She died almost as soon as I admitted her to the clinic.'

'Oh,' I said.

Later the body was shipped, by land, to Peshawar where an autopsy was performed. The strange mutilations to her hands and feet aside, and disregarding the mess that she had made of her ears, there was nothing unusual about the body.

I screwed my courage to the sticking point, and opened her kitbag. But where I expected to find Dallas's severed head, I found instead a prop, or some kind of object: metal and plastic, head shaped and with rudimentary features and a fuzz of black hair, but with yellow eyes, and pore-marked yellow skin. I handed this object over to the authorities. I've no idea what they did with it.

I went to Peshawar myself, and filed as detailed a report as I could manage. It was altogether an unusual case. Some of my superiors were minded to dismiss it: the whole thing a scam, or a mistake. Maybe Chillingworth and Dallas had holed up just outside the zone, conceivably even just inside, where the effects weren't too bad – or maybe they'd enjoyed a kind of blind luck and that was why they hadn't died. All the other stuff was too fanciful. None of it matched the satellite surveillance data. But there were people in the higher echelons who were persuaded that this was worthwhile data; or at least were persuaded that it was worth their time coming down in person to question me.

I was in a very nice Peshawar hotel, and three people came to debrief me about the whole thing: two women and one man, both much more senior that the people with whom I was used to interacting. We all sat round a table in the hotel restaurant. Coffee was served. A recording device was placed on the table, and angled to make sure it got a good rep of me.

They had read my account, of course; but they wanted me to go through the whole thing again, the story from start to finish. The man said nothing. The women would occasionally interrupt me, politely enough.

'This Ms Chillingworth,' said one, at one point. 'Was she attractive?'

'Fairly so,' I said. 'At least before she went into the Zone. Her ears looked a little strange. Late middle aged, but you know… handsome, you might say.'

'You didn't …?' When I looked startled at this question, the other woman chuckled and said: 'Rudy, your reputation precedes you, you know.'

'Not afterwards, I suppose,' said the first woman. 'But you met her several times before she went in, didn't you.'

'Nothing like that happened,' I said, trying, and I fear failing, not to blush. 'I really didn't get the vibe that she was interested in me.' I was going to add *I believe she was gay*, but there's no way a straight man can say so, especially after what I'd just expressed, without it sounding like sour grapes, or wish fulfilment: *I'd certainly have nailed her, otherwise* and so on. I held my peace.

'Her parents are both dead,' said the first woman.

'Cirrhosis,' said the second, pronouncing the word with medical crispness.

'There was some difficulty locating next of kin, in fact, to arrange the burial. Go on, with your story, please.'

I went on with my story, took it all the way to the end. The final night, the early morning bombardment – it still wasn't clear from where the shells had been fired, it seemed – Mabel slipping out of the U.N. House and later being discovered in the Babur Gardens, sunburnt and sunstruck and soon to die. 'It was a hot day, was it?'

'Not the hottest,' I said. 'But the sun can be deceptive, there. One shouldn't go out without a hat, not at midday. And sunscreen.'

'Why was she there, do you think?'

'I've really no Idea.'

'Tell us,' said the second woman, 'about the head.'

'Well, when she clonked it on the table I assumed it was the severed head of Chillingworth's companion, Dallas. To be honest, I was not eager to look inside the bag.'

'Did Chillingworth *tell* you it was Dallas's head?'

'Not in so many words, no.'

'Not in so many words?'

'I got the strong impression it was his head.'

'You got this impression from her?'

I thought back. 'I don't see where else that impression would have come from.'

'What we're trying to determine,' said the first woman, 'is whether Ms Chillingworth switched the bag, before leaving. Or whether this artefact is the same thing she carried out of the zone. And presumably into it.'

'If she ever really went into the zone,' said the second woman.

'I don't know the answer to that question,' I said. 'Though, for what it's worth, I think she did go into the zone.'

'What do *you* make the artificial head?' asked the second woman.

'It's a puzzle. It looked to me like a prop. Yellow skin and yellow-tinted eyes. Speaking as, what would you say? One of their fellowship – as a fan, I mean – I should add: you might expect it to resemble an old TV actor called Brent Spiner. But it didn't look like him. I suppose, if pressed, I would have to say it looked a *bit* like Dallas. Not much, but a bit. It has a similar head shape, I guess: wide and quite round. And the features on the artificial head are more, what's the word...? Generic than were Dallas's. Plus it obviously didn't have his colouration, or any of the modifications to his teeth or forehead. The thing was heavy, all metal and plastic. I heard there was some kind of gel where the brain should be?'

Nobody replied, so I prompted them. 'Was there?'

'There was,' said the first woman.

'And?'

'You *saw* them going into the zone?' the second woman asked. 'Chillingworth *and* Dallas both?'

'I saw them riding out of Kabul on mules. But I understand surveillance followed them into the zone, and a little way into the mountains too. Isn't that true?'

'Two people on two mules,' said the second woman. 'Maybe that was Chillingworth and Dallas. Maybe it was Chillingworth and some kind of crash-test-dummy, of which the head is the only part she brought out again. Maybe two different people altogether.'

'Rudy,' the first woman put in, 'you *believe* Chillingworth's story.'

'I believe that she believed it,' I said. 'And I suppose I believe that some of it happened. Yes.'

'That she actually went into the Zone? And came out again?'

'I do believe so. On balance, yes.'

'In which case,' the second woman asked me, 'how do *you* think she managed it?'

I'd been expecting this question, of course; but that didn't mean I knew how to answer it. 'Well,' I said, and looked at the silent man. He did not return my gaze. So I looked around the hotel restaurant, plushly empty at that time in the morning, and then through the room's tall windows across the buildings and gardens of Peshawar. The peaks of the mountains – different mountains to the ones Chillingworth had crossed, of course – rose over the tops of the town, a stone tsunami poised ever to fall and falling never.

'Well?'

'Well let's say she did go in. And Dallas, too. She told me some pretty far-fetched things, which may or may not have been hallucinations – I mean, she was perfectly aware of the possibility of hallucination I'd say, and took what steps she could to check the veracity of what she was seeing. Some of what she saw may have been figments of her imagination, perhaps under unusual conditions. But the fact that she saw weird stuff shouldn't phase us. The Afghanizone is *all* weird, wouldn't you say? Weird is the height and the breadth and the depth of that zone.'

'It's not the things she says she saw,' said the second woman said. 'It's that she survived. Forty-one people, I don't need to tell *you*, have gone into the Zone, and all of them died or lost their minds. Why should she be the one person not to suffer that fate?'

'We know the zone is capricious,' pointed out the first woman. 'Maybe this is just another caprice.'

'With respect,' said the second woman, 'insofar as capricious implies a governing intellect, we don't know anything of the sort.'

'I've been thinking about it, obviously,' I said. 'Chillingworth believed that the zone is something caused by extra-terrestrial activity. I know that's not a theory with a lot of *official* traction …'

'Indeed,' said the second woman, in a deep voice.

'But she believed it. And she believed that by dressing up as a science fiction alien she would *placate* whatever powers were behind the zone.'

'It's hard to credit that she really believed that,' said the second woman. 'As if there's a little green person, sitting in an invisible surveillance bubble over the middle of Kafiristan, who is saying, oh, that human being is dressed in standard twenty-first century clothing, she must die, ah, but these two are dressed as characters from an old science fiction television show – they get to live.'

'Presumably that's not how it happened,' I said. 'But, you know. Who knows? Chillingworth strongly suggested that her survival, and Dallas's survival, depended upon the strength of belief with which they inhabited their roles. If they genuinely believed themselves alien, they did better. When their faith faltered, the Zone began to turn on them. The way Chillingworth told it, Dallas died because he went full meta on his role-playing, starting critiquing the underlying show… He lost the purity of faith that inhabits true cosplay.'

'Play,' said the second woman. 'Like children?'

'Children have an unexamined wisdom about play,' I said. 'They don't self-consciously *pretend* to play; they just play. They enter wholeheartedly into the role, the game. Kids are better at play than adults. Maybe that's what this is about.'

'Doesn't seem very likely,' said the second woman. And the first added, 'It would be hard to justify sending volunteers into a probably fatal environment with the advice that they should *play* their way through, like little children.'

'Well, when you put it like that,' I agreed.

At this point the man made his one and only contribution to our discussion. He spoke, with a higher-pitched, rather more flute-like voice than I would have expected from his long, seamed face. He said, 'I say to you, except ye become as little children, ye shall not enter into the kingdom of heaven.'

The women ignored this. 'Maybe the zone was placated, as you say, or otherwise bamboozled by these two pretending to be alien life forms,' said the first. 'Or maybe it was something else.'

'Or maybe it was nothing,' said the second woman.

'Maybe the zone is more interested in stories than science,' I offered. 'The other observers who have tried to penetrate it have been scientists, yes? Well maybe that's where we've been going wrong. These two were dressed as characters from a TV show first broadcast forty-and-some years ago. So what if the Zone is the product of aliens, from a world forty-light-years away and they came here not to meet us but because they were really big fans of …'

'I don't believe this to be a fruitful line of enquiry,' said the second woman, briskly.

There was an embarrassed silence. Then the first woman said, 'Is there anything else?'

'There's one other issue,' I said. 'The zone Chillingworth says she passed through was uninhabited, which is what we would expect. Uninhabited by human beings, I mean. Corpses, yes; but no live people. Then again, she was clear that there were other... things. Some of those were, she said, like flying demons or monsters. But many more were tech. She was clearly talking about really high-spec technological devices – swarming drones. Maybe future tech?'

All three were looking at me.

'Rudy,' said the second woman, with a warning tone. 'Don't make a fool of yourself.'

'Well,' said the first woman, briskly, as if there were nothing more to say. She got to her feet. 'Thank you, Rudy. You have been... helpful.'

When she got up, the other two got up as well, and of course I followed.

'Can I ask?' I asked. 'Do you happen to know where the head is now?'

'In a research facility somewhere' said the first woman. 'California, I believe.'

And there the matter rests.

Five

Except that, of course, it doesn't rest. It is the opposite of restful. I've hardly had a whole night's sleep since Chillingworth came back from the zone. It's the dreams. They keep waking me up. Now, I know there's little more boring in this our sublunary world than hearing other people recite their dreams, so I guess I'm craving your indulgence. Maybe they'll do some research on the head that will reveal all, and release the news to the world. I'm not holding my breath on that. Maybe they'll finally locate the command centre from the zone – assuming it has one – and bomb it to crumbs and dust and that'll be that. I figure they're trying to bomb a place, when what they need to be doing is bombing a time, or a state of mind, or an abstract concept. I don't know. When I kept waking up, breathless (I'm not holding my breath because I have no breath to hold) and sweating and thirsty, I'd say: it's the climate here. It's the snafu'd air-con. But I was rotated to a posting in Glasgow, and I'm still doing it. Waking up stare-eyed. I've gone from never remembering my dreams to being unable to forget them.

I'm there. They're there. Suppose they sweltered here three thousand years patient for our destruction? I see Dallas' back as he strides off, and the bursting geometric pattern the sunlight makes me think I'm looking through a camera lens, rather than through my eyes. To act can be decisive, but there is a greeting beyond the act. There's an ox, I think, which may be more Indian than Afghani: lugging the earth, hauling ploughlines through the solid world so that there's grain to eat next year. And it is this big brown ox that speaks to me: 'one day the zone will disappear,' it says, giving me the side-eye because it can't give me any other kind of eye. I can feel the heat falling on me hard, and the light dazzling mine eyes. Mine eyes, thine eyes. 'I'm not sure I believe that,' I tell the ox, but already I'm feeling that bat-flutter inside my ribcage, and sweat is pinning and needling my skin, and I feel the gut-panic. I want to wake up, and I can't yet wake up. But why should the prospect of the zone vanishing *alarm* me? Wouldn't that be a consummation devoutly to be wished? I mean, wouldn't it? Life could go back to the way it was before, except that obviously it couldn't, and wouldn't. The future would be haunted by the past, and more to the point, the future would be haunted by the past's dream of the future. Isn't that the whole point of the zone? Its weirdnesses and dangers, its glamour and strength? The weird reweaving of time and cause-effect and threat and so on? What would be left? The odd artefact, maybe. Echoes in the rooms of the world, where women and men stop for a moment, and stretch their spines with a hand on one hip, and turn their heads just enough to the right to see through the window, all in unison, and gaze without even really registering it over the rooftops, fishscaled with tiles, slick with sun-shine as if wet, and the drones in the air, and the birds in the trees, and the distant irregular line of the horizon. At any rate the Ox is having none of this nonsense, and says, 'man, one day the zone will vanish, and at that moment you will finally understand what the zone is.' That thought fills me with an acid sense of dread, sifting through my torso, and I start to cry out, no, no, it's not there to be understood. And the Ox speaks for a third time and says: you can understand with your head and you can understand with your heart and there is a third mode of understanding …' And the beast says nothing more, because nothing more needs to be said. But I don't like it. *What do you mean?* I shout. Depending on the dream, I might shout different things, but the emotional freight is always the same: panic and anger and a deep sense of revulsion. So for instance, I might shout: *what do you* mean, *the future will be haunted by the past's dream of the future? What does that even mean?* That would be when I wake up, usually. Anxious and sweat-wet and panting. Gasping. It's a very *untidy* sort of sound, gasping. Don't you think?

I don't have to wait until the zone disappears, assuming it ever disappears, to know what the zone is. I know what the zone is, now. So do you, the you who is reading thing. How can you not?

About the Author

Adam Roberts is the author of twenty novels, most recently *By the Pricking of Her Thumb* (Gollancz 2018) and *The Black Prince* (with Anthony Burgess, Unbound 2018). He has a day job, teaching English and Creative Writing at Royal Holloway, University of London, and lives in the easternmost spur of Berkshire with his wife and family. He considers Rudyard Kipling the finest writer of short stories in English.

NewCon Press Novellas Set 5: The Alien Among Us

Nomads – Dave Hutchinson

Are there really refugees from another time living among us? And, if so, what dreadful event are they fleeing from? When a high speed car chase leads Police Sergeant Frank Grant to Dronfield Farm, he finds himself the focus of unwanted attention from Internal Affairs and is confronted by questions he's not sure he ever wants to hear answered.

Morpho – Philip Palmer

When the corpse on the mortuary slab sits up and speaks to Hayley, asking for her help, she thinks she's losing her mind. If only it were that simple… Philip Palmer delivers a tense fast-paced tale of a secret society that governs our world from the shadows, of immortality at a terrible price and events that lead to the overthrow of social order.

The Man Who Would Be Kling – Adam Roberts

When two people ask the manager at Kabul Station to take them into the Afghanizone he refuses. What sane person wouldn't? Said to represent alien visitation, the zone is deadly. Nothing works there. Electrical items malfunction or simply blow up. The pair go in anyway, and the biggest surprise is when one of them walks out again. Nobody survives the zone, so how has she?

Macsen Against the Jugger – Simon Morden

Two centuries after the Earth fell to alien machines known as the Visitors, humanity survives in sparse nomadic tribes. Macsen is an adventurer, undertaking hazardous quests to please Hona Loy. Macsen never fails, but this time he is pitted against a deadly Jugger. Can he somehow survive, or will it fall to his faithful companion Laylaw to tell the tale of his noble death?

NewCon Press Novellas

Released in sets of four, each novella is an independent stand-alone story. Each set is linked by shared cover art, split between the books, providing separate covers that link to form a single image greater than the parts.

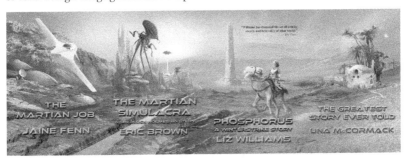

Set 1: Science Fiction
Novellas by Alastair Reynolds, Simon Morden, Anne Charnock, Neil Williamson. Cover art by Chris Moore

Set 2: Dark Thrillers
Novellas by Simon Clark, Alison Littlewood, Sarah Lotz, Jay Caselberg.
Cover art by Vincent Sammy

Set 3: The Martian Quartet
Novellas by Jaine Fenn, Eric Brown, Liz Williams, Una McCormack.
Cover art by Jim Burns

Set 4: Strange Tales
Novellas by Gary Gibson, Adam Roberts, Ricardo Pinto, Hal Duncan.
Cover art by Ben Baldwin

Set 5: The Alien Among Us
Novellas by Dave Hutchinson, Philip Palmer, Adam Roberts, Simon Morden.
Cover art by Peter Hollinghurst

Each novella is available separately in paperback or as a limited numbered hardback edition, signed by the author. Each set is available as a strictly limited lettered slipcase set, containing all four of the books as signed dust-jacketed hardbacks and featuring the combined artwork as a wrap-around.

www.newconpress.co.uk

IMMANION PRESS

Purveyors of Speculative Fiction

www.immanion-press.com

Vivia by Tanith Lee

Tanith Lee was writing grimdark fantasy even before it was known as a genre. Gritty, savage and darkly erotic, *Vivia* is one of the author's darkest - and finest - works. Vivia, the neglected daughter of a vicious warlord, discovers strange, lightless caverns deep beneath her father's castle. Here she finds an entity she believes is a living god and, in her loneliness, seeks its favour. After war and disease devastate her father's lands, Vivia is taken captive by the hedonistic Prince Zulgaris and kept as his concubine. In this barbaric land, where life means very little, and the spectre of the plague haunts the alleys and markets of even the greatest city, circumstances can change very quickly. No life is safe, and treachery abounds. Perhaps, in such a brutal world, only remote pitiless creatures like Vivia can survive unscathed. But at what cost? ISBN: 978-1-907737-98-5 £12.99 $16.99

Songs to Earth and Sky edited by Storm Constantine

Six writers explore the eight seasonal festivals of the year, dreaming up new beliefs and customs, new myths, new dehara – the gods of Wraeththu. As different communities develop among Wraeththu, the androgynous race who have inherited a ravaged earth, so fresh legends spring up – or else ghosts from the inception of their kind come back to haunt them. From the silent, snow-heavy forests of Megalithican mountains, through the lush summer fields of Alba Sulh, into the hot, shimmering continent of Olathe, this book explores the Wheel of the Year, bringing its powerful spirits and landscapes to vivid life. Nine brand new tales, including a novella, a novelette and a short story from Storm herself, and stories from *Wendy Darling, Nerine Dorman, Suzanne Gabriel, Fiona Lane* and *E. S. Wynn*. ISBN 978-1-907737-84-8 £11.99 $15.50 pbk

Lightning Source UK Ltd.
Milton Keynes UK
UKHW040639170222
398838UK00001B/157